JOHANN WOLFGANG VON GOETHE

The Sufferings of Young Werther

A New Translation by Stanley Corngold

W. W. NORTON & COMPANY

NEW YORK | LONDON

For information about permission to reproduce selections from this book,
write to Permissions, W. W. Norton & Company, Inc.,
500 Fifth Avenue, New York, NY 10110

For information about special discounts for bulk purchases, please
contact W. W. Norton Special Sales at specialsales@wwnorton.com
or 800-233-4830

Manufacturing by RR Donnelley, Harrisonburg
Book design by Brooke Koven
Production manager: Julia Druskin

Library of Congress Cataloging-in-Publication Data

Goethe, Johann Wolfgang von, 1749–1832.
[Werther. English]
The sufferings of young Werther / Johann Wolfgang von Goethe ; a new
translation by Stanley Corngold. — 1st ed.
p. cm.
ISBN 978-0-393-07938-8 (hardcover)
1. Young men—Psychology—Fiction. 2. Unrequited love—Fiction.
3. Despair—Fiction. 4. Loss (Psychology)—Fiction.
I. Corngold, Stanley. II. Title.
PT2027.W3C67 2012
833'.6—dc23
2011029508

W. W. Norton & Company, Inc.
500 Fifth Avenue, New York, N.Y. 10110
www.wwnorton.com

W. W. Norton & Company Ltd.
Castle House, 75/76 Wells Street, London W1T 3QT

1 2 3 4 5 6 7 8 9 0

⚜CONTENTS⚜

TRANSLATOR'S
INTRODUCTION

YOUNG GOETHE wrote *The Sufferings of Young Werther* in four weeks in spring 1774, a hot outpouring of genius; the book was swiftly printed and sold at the Leipzig fair that fall. If it was thrilling for this twenty-five-year-old footloose lawyer and dilettante to know that his novel was being bought, pirated, read, translated, and imitated throughout Europe, it was to become a burden as he matured into *Privy Councillor Johann Wolfgang von Goethe*—diplomat, scientist, literary giant, and maker of prudent maxims; forever after, Goethe was to be known as the author of *Young Werther* and identified with his suicidal hero. Goethe saw this danger early and furnished a second edition in 1775 with a poem that ends in italic, "Be a man, and do not follow me [to my doom]." The danger was real, as Goethe himself acknowledged: Werther "is a creation . . . that I, like the pelican, fed with the blood of my own heart. . . . I am uneasy when I look at it and dread the return of the pathological condition from which it sprang." At the end of his life, he spoke ruefully of the novel's "fire rockets" that continued to flare up in and around him for half a century.

Werther is himself—this self-absorbed, provincial youth in a German novel. At the same time he anticipates a recurring type: the late-adolescent, elite-educated, hormone-besotted, rebellious youth with artistic inclinations who would rather be in love—and who then promptly falls in love with the wrong woman. But Werther would not seize our imagination now were it not for his "gift," as Goethe wrote, "for profound and pure feeling and true penetration." And once created and given voice, what a gifted presenter of himself this Werther is! As readers, we wrestle with the paradox of how someone—Werther—can claim to be so lost, so disconsolate, so barren of speech and feeling and yet find his way to the words that make his struggle unforgettable. At the end, of course, Goethe needs to have the Editor step in for Werther, to give an account of a disintegrating character in a different sort of language—a pedantic, official-sounding, propriety-upholding language—implying that Werther was no longer able to speak for himself. But even here, when Werther's letters and notebooks are quoted, his words remain vivid and gripping even as he laments.

For much of the novel, Werther cannot find his way; his thoughts, his longings, his talents exceed anything he thinks the world can offer him as a worthwhile object of pursuit, and at times we may be inclined to agree. True, that worthy object might be his beloved Lotte, but she is by definition unavailable; she is engaged to another, a deserving man. For the rest, work in government, at the ambassador's office, is a plague, dry as dust and continually checked and interfered with by that dreaded figure, one's "superior." Entry into aristocratic society is soon enough proved fruitless—and humiliating—when Werther, a *bourgeois,* thoughtlessly wanders into it. There is art—in the beginning Werther seems to be a capable draughtsman—but soon his talents fail him; in this case, the object of his art, Nature, is an object not too small but too big; he is prone to be overwhelmed by landscape—by hills and peaks and floods. And here, where Nature has ceased to be the object of the painter's masterful art, it can become a demon too, offering, in its domination of the individual mind, a tempting alternative to consciousness: *un*consciousness, ecstasy, self-loss. Franz Kafka, whose work is shot through with reminiscences of *Werther*—and who admitted his dependence on Goethe—wrote of the life-task: "not to shunt off the ego but consume it," which defines the artist's task especially: to seize all the ego's energies, longings, hurts, passions and burn them as fuel for the higher project— the work of art. This is Goethe's view and Goethe's task but not one that Werther can perform; the declared object of his art is Nature, and Nature is too chaotic, a provocation to shake off the self in death—the bigger ecstasy. And this is what, in the end, Goethe deplores and writes his *Werther* to steel himself against—the dreadful vision, as in Werther's great letter of August 18, 1771, of "the spectacle of infinite life transformed before my eyes into the abyss of an ever open grave."

The text that follows is a *translation,* an effortful attempt to capture the always astonishing liveliness of Goethe's language. Like the best wines of those years, it still keeps its fruit, its freshness—it breathes, it lives. For if *Werther* is an event for Goethe the writer, a breakthrough into a career as a literary hero, it is much more: it is a breakthrough for German literary language. You cannot find an earlier German literary work that displays such a range of subjective experience in words that are transparent to this experience and arranged in so convincing a word order. *Werther* marks an achievement of truly world-historical proportions: in this furnace of linguistic activity, we see the modern German literary language being forged. Goethe's novel became a constant source of inspiration to younger contemporaries, glorious in their German prose, such as Friedrich Hölderlin, the author of another great epistolary novel—*Hyperion*—that richly repays reading today, not to mention the more familiar, grand inheritors, such as Nietzsche, Thomas Mann, Kafka.

Mann is especially worth noting for *Werther*-lovers as the author of *Lotte in Weimar*, a magical reconstruction of a visit many decades later by Charlotte Kestner née Buff, the model of Werther's Lotte, to Weimar, the residence of the mature and very grand person Werther had become. This is Privy Councillor von Goethe, the Duke's right hand. In Mann's imagination, Lotte and Goethe do not meet; Goethe keeps his distance from her, although in historical fact he did invite her to dinner. Nonetheless, in Mann's account, we have a sign of Goethe's strenuous distancing of himself from Werther's passion, beginning, of course, with the heightened role of the lawyerly Editor in Book II of the novel and then the fine adjustments of tone in the "definitive" edition of 1787, which is the basis of this translation.

In early days, in 1775, Goethe had depicted the inaccessible Charlotte Buff as an object worthy of throwing a young man into a life-and-world-denying frenzy. She is adorable. It was easier for Goethe to generate a proper distance in 1816, when, in the words of his soul mate, another Charlotte— Charlotte von Stein—he was "recently visited by Lotte from *The Sufferings of Werther*, Mrs. Kestner from Hanover. [. . .] She is pleasant company, but of course no Werther would shoot himself anymore for her."

But none of these retrospective withdrawals of sympathy have been able to extinguish in readers the most immediate relation to, and love of, Werther—especially in Book I— dashing in his buff-colored trousers and vest, high boots, and blue frock coat. Certainly not Napoleon, who, on Goethe's

visit to him in Erfurt in 1808, declared that he had read the novel seven times. Furthermore, as proof of the fact, Napoleon produced an allegedly profound analysis of the novel, including one objection. In certain passages (which we leave to the reader to discover), he minded Goethe's mingling two motives as causes of his hero's death: passionate love and also frustrated ambition. This entanglement, declared Napoleon, was not "true to nature" and diminished the reader's impression of the overpowering influence on Werther of his unrequited love. "Why did you do that?" Napoleon asked, whereupon Goethe, always the practical diplomat, had an answer. A writer, he replied, might be excused for employing a trick from time to time in order to bring about effects he did not feel able to produce in a direct and natural way. What Goethe was declaring with this excuse to Napoleon was the *German* author's independence of French models of strict unity in exposition; Goethe's early model was Shakespeare and not the great French dramatists Racine and Corneille. Furthermore, Goethe *meant* to portray the grief of the sons of the bourgeoisie at the spiritless, joyless prospect of the empty activity available to them in the Germany of their time. "In a fit of morose arrogance," such people, as he drily wrote, might very well "become acquainted with the thought that if life no longer suited them, they could in any case, and as they wished, take leave of it."

Werther produces an effect of spontaneous genius, but it remains remarkable how beautifully structured it is. It is divided into two "Books"—a Book One full of some hope and joy, set in early 1771, and a Book Two full of increasing melancholy and doom, ending in 1772. Werther's growing despair is correlated with a wintry season: he shoots himself on the verge of Christmas, in a gesture full of overdetermined meaning. He has repeatedly likened his grief to that of Christ; that grief is deeply, darkly exaggerated by his refusing the gesture of hope accompanying Christ's birth; but, as he repeatedly declares, Christ's death is also the promise of a higher life, and in this way Werther suggests that his death is also an entry into a higher sphere, in which he hopes to find his beloved Lotte again—and her mother and Albert only secondarily.

Again and again his dire end is forecast, plainly and symbolically: early on he speaks of the freedom that is reserved for every man and woman, for one can choose to leave this earthly prison. In a symbolic sense, Werther's sudden perception, as early as Book I, of Nature as a monster forever devouring and regurgitating its own creatures points toward his own wild moods and suicidal impulses. His swapping his beloved Homer's famous luminousness and celebration of life for the (apocryphal) works of a gloomy, death-drunk Gaelic poet called Ossian forecasts a downward drift of the spirit. Werther identifies his own plight with a madman and a murderer, both of whom he defends, but here his generosity of spirit seems tainted by what is called *nostalgie de la boue*, the ascription of higher spiritual value to social outcasts and derelicts.

This foreshadowing of his own doom through identification with the doomed has the effect of driving forward the reader's attention to Werther's fate: it is part of the general onward-rushing character of the entire story. This thrust forward, almost impatience, is a feature of Werther's character as well as of his language. From time to time he sets up elaborate rhetorical constructions marked by periodic rhythm, but he cannot end them properly. More noticeable is his habit of merely writing the word "and" between two moments of perception that are actually opposed and normally call for an expression signaling this opposition, such as "but" or "while" or "on the other hand." The reader is left to intuit the contrast. Other translations supply the oppositional word where logic seems to call for it; the present translation does not; the book's associative, paratactic rush makes a point. Werther is, by his own admission, "restless and unfortunate," and so is his style restless and unfortunate from the standpoint of the requirements of logic. The pattern of his writing is the punctual equivalence of moments of experience—and subordination be damned. It is not— good Lord!—that Werther lacks the evolved intelligence or the linguistic maturity capable of hypotaxis, that is, the regular use of well-structured subordinate clauses—he has had a classical education and he is well-informed about the technical jargon of aesthetics in his day; but his rush past logic is expressive of the irrational drive that hurls him from one totally gripping emotional-intellectual instant to the next.

In translating *Werther,* I have held to the principle that I sketched out in my translation of *Kafka's Selected Stories* published as a Norton Critical Edition. It is enunciated by John Donne in 1624, soon after a team of forty-seven scholars had finished their work, in 1611, of translating canonical Greek, Hebrew, and Latin texts into what was to be called the King James Bible. Donne wrote: "God employs several translators." It is with some hesitation, of course, that one evokes the idea of translating *Werther* under the head of translating the Word of God, since Goethe, great as he is, is by common consent the lesser writer. Still, *The Sufferings of Young Werther* is very great, a greatness in fact owed in good part to its personal— and even heretical—deployment of biblical language and Christian ideas; and indeed it even served as the bible to the many young men and women in the late eighteenth century who imitated the thought and style of Werther and Lotte— and to the dozen or so who imitated Werther's death.

My translation principle requires me to translate each page "cold" and then, after many passes, consult the many other extant translations. For it is my firm belief that translators should stand on the shoulders of their predecessors. We are, after all, a collective—translators and readers alike; we are one community in our devotion to the most truthful possible understanding of the works of this master writer, an understanding that in every case involves a personal "rewriting" of the text. If one were writing an essay on *Werther*, would one make a point of never consulting any previous writer who had written on *Werther*? Of course not. And should one as a translator fail to consult any or all previous translations of *Werther*? Of course not. But then the question of the originality of one's reading or writing about the author could arise. There is a well-documented practice in the matter of attributing phrases and formulations cited from the works of previous writers: you footnote them. And what is the right thing to do if as a translator you encounter in a previous translation a rendering that is straightforwardly better than your own? Ignore this knowledge for the sake of a putative absolute originality? No. But how can you indicate your debt now and again to your inspired predecessor? You cannot footnote this or that phrase. And so here I wish to compose a blanket dedication to the predecessors whose work has, in the words once more of Kafka, "refreshed, satisfied, liberated, and exalted me" and I hope you too, reader. Chief among them are Stanley Applebaum, Catherine Hutter, Victor Lange, Elizabeth Mayer and Louise Bogan, Clark Muenzer, Burton Pike, and Harry Steinhauer.

In saying that I have not hesitated on occasion to employ the locutions of other translators when they seemed better than my own, I should note, in this vexed matter of "originality," that all too often, with both delight and despair, I found I had hit upon exactly the same formulations as my predecessors. That is inevitably the case, because Goethe's syntax is usually quite clear, his word choice is not recherché, and key words recur. Again and again, there are simply no two ways about it. In one important respect, the text lends itself to literal English translation: this is the above-mentioned factor of parataxis, the direct, forward-moving, "and . . . and" structure of Werther's thought. And here we confront once more the major drive of the work itself, so distinctive as a full, phenomenologically saturated presentation of a self informed by the most intense desire to annihilate itself. This tension dictates the widest task of the translator: to find a language at once Apollonian—firmly delineated, intelligent, full of light and enlightenment—and Dionysian—dark, death-driven—a concept employed by Nietzsche, Goethe's great admirer, in thinking about him. Some of this darkness might be conveyed by an impression of foreignness now and again in this translation, the result of following the German text very closely and never knowingly choosing to use a word that was not current in English ca. 1787.

You find the claim, here and there in the critical literature, that the language and style of *Werther* has long ceased to be a model for anything a twenty-first-century writer would write. It may have captivated his contemporaries and Nietzsche and even Mann and Kafka, but that was then. I was prepared to believe this claim until I came across this passage in a work by an eminent contemporary novelist, the Nobel Prize–winning J. M. Coetzee. In his autobiographical novel *Youth*, published in 2002, we find this description of the hero:

> Tired out, one Sunday afternoon, he folds his jacket into a pillow, stretches out on the greensward, and sinks into a sleep or half-sleep in which consciousness does not vanish but continues to hover. It is a state he has not known before: in his very blood he seems to feel the steady wheeling of the earth. The faraway cries of children, the birdsong, the whirr of insects gather force and come together in a paean of joy. His heart swells.

At last! he thinks. At last it has come, the moment of ecstatic unity with the All! Fearful that the moment will slip away, he tries to put a halt to the clatter of thought, tries simply to be a conduit for the great universal force that has no name.

Thus are the detractors of *Werther*'s perennial influence confuted.

Stanley Corngold
Berlin, January 2011

The Sufferings of
Young Werther

I have diligently collected everything I could discover about the story of poor Werther and set it before you here, knowing that you will thank me for it. You will not be able to withhold your admiration and love for his spirit and character or your tears for his fate.

And you, good soul, who feel the same urgency as he, take comfort from his sufferings and let this little book be your friend if by fate or your own fault you can find none closer to you.

~ BOOK ONE ~

HOW HAPPY I am to be away! Dearest friend, what a thing it is, the human heart! To leave you, whom I love so much, from whom I was inseparable, and yet to be happy! I know you will forgive me. Weren't my other attachments especially chosen by fate just to torment a heart like mine? Poor Leonore! And yet I was innocent. Was it my fault that while her sister's willful charms were keeping me so pleasantly entertained, passion formed in her poor heart? And yet—am I entirely innocent? Didn't I nourish her feelings? Didn't I delight in those genuine expressions of her nature that so often made us laugh, though they were not laughable at all? Didn't I—oh what is man that he is allowed to complain about himself! I will, my dear friend, I promise you, I will improve, I will not chew over the bit of woe that fate presents us with, the way I have always done; I will enjoy the present and let bygones be bygones. Certainly, you're right, dearest friend, there would be less pain among men if—God knows why they're constructed so!—they did not so busily employ their bustling imagination to summon up memories of old woes rather than accept an indifferent present.

Please be so good as to tell my mother that I am conducting her business as best I can and that I will soon be sending her news. I have spoken to my aunt and have found her not at all the evil woman she was made out to be. She is a lively, excitable person with a heart of gold. I explained my mother's concern about the portion of the inheritance that was withheld; she told me her reasons, the causes, and under what conditions she was prepared to give up all of it, more than we asked for.—In short, I don't feel like writing about it now; tell my mother that everything is bound to turn out well. And, my dear friend, once again I have learned from this little piece of business that misunderstandings and neglect may cause more confusion in the world than do cunning and malice. At any rate, the last two are certainly more rare.

For the rest, I feel altogether well here. Solitude in this paradisiacal place is a precious balm to my heart, and this season of youth, with its abundance, warms my often-shuddering heart. Every tree, every hedge is a bouquet of blossoms and makes you want to turn into a May bug, so as to float in this sea of fragrances and draw all your nourishment from it.

The town itself is unpleasant; by contrast, it is surrounded by inexpressible natural beauty. This moved the late Count von M. to plant a garden on one of the hills that intersect one another in the most beautiful variety, forming the loveliest valleys. The garden is simple, and immediately on entering you sense that the plan was designed not by a scientific gardener but by a feeling heart that intended to enjoy itself here. I have already shed more than one tear for the deceased in the ruined little arbor that was his favorite spot and now is mine. Soon I will be the master of the garden; I enjoy the gardener's favor even after only these few days, and he will not have done badly as a result.

MAY 10

A wonderful gaiety has seized my entire soul, like the sweet spring mornings I wholeheartedly enjoy. I am alone and glad to be alive in this place, which is made for souls like mine. I am so happy, dearest friend, so deeply immersed in the sense of calm existence that my art is suffering. I could not draw now, not a single stroke, and yet I have never been a greater painter than in these moments. When the vapor of this lovely valley rises around me and the midday sun rests on the impenetrable dark of my woods and only a few stray gleams steal into the inner sanctuary, then I lie in the high grass by the tumbling brook, and closer to the earth a thousand different little shoots grow distinct before my eyes; when closer to my heart I feel the teeming of the little world between the blades of grass, the countless, unfathomable shapes of the tiny worms, the tiny gnats, and feel the presence of the Almighty Who created us in His image, the breath of the All-loving Who in eternal bliss holds us hovering and keeps us; my friend! when the light fades around my eyes and the world around me and the heavens rest in my soul like the shape of a beloved—then I often yearn and think: Oh, could you express that, could you breathe into the paper everything that lives with such warmth and fullness in you that it might become the mirror of your soul, the way your soul is the mirror of unending God—my friend—but I am dying of this, I succumb to the force of the splendor of these displays.

MAY 12

I do not know whether deceitful spirits hover around this region or whether it is the warm, divine fantasy in my heart that makes everything around me appear like paradise. Just outside the town there is a well, a well that holds me spellbound like Melusine and her sisters.—You walk down a little hill and find yourself before a stone vault from which some twenty steps go down to where the clearest water spurts from marble blocks. The low wall above, which forms the surrounding enclosure, the tall trees that cast their shade all around, the coolness of the place; all this has something so attractive, so awesome about it. Not a day goes by that I do not sit there for an hour. The girls come from the town to fetch water, the most innocent occupation and the most essential, which in olden times the daughters of kings performed. When I sit there, the patriarchal idea comes to life so vividly around me; they are there, all our forebears, meeting others and courting at the well, while benevolent spirits hover over the fountains and the springs. Oh, anyone who does not experience the same feeling can never have refreshed himself at the coolness of the well after a strenuous walk on a summer day.

MAY 13

You ask me whether you should send me my books.—My dear, for God's sake, I beg you, keep them away from me! I no longer want to be influenced, encouraged, inspired: this heart of mine rages enough by itself. I need a lullaby, and I have found that abundantly in my Homer. How often do I lull my rebellious blood to rest, for you have never seen anything so irregular, so impatient as this heart of mine. My dear, do I need to tell you, you who have so often been burdened with watching me swing from sorrow to ecstasy and from sweet melancholy to destructive passion? And I treat my little heart like a sick child; its every wish is granted. Don't repeat what I say; there are people who would hold it against me.

MAY 15

The simple people of the town know me already and are fond of me, especially the children. At first, when I would go up to them and ask them in a friendly way about this and that, some of them thought I was making fun of them and dismissed me quite rudely. I didn't let that bother me; but I felt very strongly something I've often noticed: persons of standing will always keep coldly distant from the common people, as if they were afraid to lose something through intimacy; and then there are those flighty creatures and nasty jokers who pretend to descend to their level in order to make these poor commoners feel their superiority all the more keenly.

I know well enough that we are not all equal nor can we be; but I believe that the person who feels it necessary to keep aloof from the so-called rabble in order to maintain his dignity is just as reprehensible as the coward who hides from his enemy lest he be defeated.

Not long ago I came to the well and found a young servant girl who had put her jug on the lowest step and was looking around to see whether a friend might come to help her lift it onto her head. I went down the steps and looked at her.—Would you like me to help you, my girl? I said.— She blushed deeply.—Oh no, sir! she said.—Let's not stand on ceremony!—She adjusted her head cushion, and I helped her. She thanked me, and up the stairs she went.

I've made all sorts of acquaintances but as yet I have not found any real companionship. I do not know what it is about me that attracts others; so many of them like me and attach themselves to me, and then it hurts me when we walk only a short way together. If you want to know what the people here are like, I have to tell you: like people everywhere! The human race—it's a uniform thing. Most people spend the greatest part of the time struggling to stay alive, and the little bit of freedom they have left makes them so anxious that they'll look for any means to get rid of it. Oh, it is the lot of mankind!

But these are a very good kind of people! When at times I forget myself, at times enjoy with them the pleasures that are still granted to us humans—to joke and have fun openly and lightheartedly at a well-laid table, to arrange an outing or a dance and that kind of thing at just the right moment—all that has quite a good effect on me; only it must not occur to me that so many other forces lie dormant in me, all rotting away unused, which I must carefully conceal. Oh, it so constricts my heart.—And yet! to be misunderstood: that is the fate of our sort.

Alas, that the friend of my youth has gone! Alas, that I ever knew her!—I would say: you are a fool, you are looking for something that cannot be found on earth. But she was mine; I felt that heart, that great soul in whose presence I seemed to myself to be more than I was because I was everything I could be. Good God! At that time was there a single force in my soul left unused? Wasn't I able to unfold before her all the wonderful emotion with which my heart embraces nature? Wasn't our time together an endless weave of the subtlest feeling, the sharpest wit, whose variations even to the point of misbehavior bore the stamp of genius? And now!—Oh, her years that were a few more than mine led her to the grave before me. I shall never forget her, her steady mind and her divine tolerance.

A few days ago I made the acquaintance of V., an open-hearted young man with a pleasing set of features. He has just left the university, does not consider himself wise, and yet thinks that he knows more than others. He was diligent too, as I can tell from various signs; in short, he has a nice little store of knowledge. When he heard that I sketched a great deal and knew Greek (two sensations in this part of the country), he came to see me and unloaded his store of knowledge, from Batteau to Wood, from de Piles to Winckelmann, and assured me that he had read the first volume of Sulzer's *Theory* from beginning to end and owned a manuscript by Heyne on the study of antiquity. I did not argue with him.

I have met another good man, the Prince's district officer, a frank, guileless person. I'm told that it fills one's soul with pleasure to see him with his children, of whom there are nine; people make a great to-do especially about his oldest daughter. He has invited me to visit him, and I will do so the first day I can. He lives in one of the Prince's hunting lodges, an hour and a half from here, where he received permission to move after the death of his wife, since it was too painful for him to live at his official residence in town.

Otherwise, I've run across a couple of convoluted eccentrics, about whom everything is unendurable, the most unbearable being their demonstrations of friendship.

Farewell! You will like this letter, it is entirely factual.

MAY 22

That human life is but a dream is something that has already occurred to many, and this feeling forever haunts me as well. When I observe the narrow limits in which man's powers of action and investigation are confined; when I see how all our activity aims at satisfying needs that once again have no purpose beyond prolonging our wretched existence; and that all our satisfaction with certain aspects of our investigations is only dreamy resignation, since we merely paint colored shapes and brilliant prospects on the walls that hold us captive—all this, Wilhelm, stuns me into silence. I turn back into myself and discover a world! Once again, more as intuition and dim craving than as distinct imagery and vital force. And then everything swims before my senses, and I go on, smiling dreamily into the world.

That children do not know why they want things—on this all high and mightily learned schoolmasters and tutors agree; but that, like children, adults also stumble through the world and, like children, do not know whence they come and whither they go, nor act to some true purpose any more than children do, and like them are ruled by cookies and cakes and birch rods—no one likes to think that, and yet to me it is palpable truth.

I'm quite willing to admit—because I know what you're likely to want to say to me here, that those people are happiest who, like children, live for the moment, wander about with their dolls, dressing and undressing them, and keep a sharp eye on the cupboard where Mama has locked up the pastries, and when they finally get what they want, stuff their mouths with them and cry: More!—Those are happy creatures. And those others, too, are happy who give grand names to their paltry occupations or even to their passions and present them to the human race as gigantic accomplishments for its welfare and salvation.—Happy are they who can live this way! But those who in all humility realize the sum total, who see how neatly every contented citizen can shape his little garden into a paradise, and how tirelessly even the merest wretch, panting, makes his way beneath his burden, all of them

equally determined to see the light of the sun one minute longer—yes, that man keeps still, and he creates his world out of himself, and he is happy as well because he is human. And then, confined as he is, he still always keeps in his heart the sweet sense of freedom, knowing that he can leave this prison whenever he chooses.

MAY 26

You've long known my habit of planting myself down, setting up a little hut at some cozy spot, and settling in there in the simplest manner. Here, too, I've once again come across a spot that attracted me.

About an hour's ride from town there is a village called Wahlheim.† Its situation on a hill is enthralling, and if you go farther along on the footpath to the village, you get a sudden view over the entire valley. At the inn a good woman, pleasant and sprightly despite her age, sells wine, beer, and coffee; and what tops everything are two linden trees whose widespread limbs cover the little square in front of the church, which is surrounded by peasant cottages, barns, and homesteads. I have rarely found a spot so cozy, so homey, and I have my little table brought out from the inn, and my chair, drink my coffee there, and read my Homer. The first time, when one fine afternoon I chanced upon the spot under the linden trees, I found the place deserted. Everyone was out in the fields except a boy of about four who sat on the ground, holding an infant of about six months that sat between his feet; he was clasping the child to his chest with both arms, so that he served as a sort of armchair, and despite the liveliness with

† The reader need not go to the trouble of locating the village named above; it was considered necessary to change the real names found in the original. (Note by Goethe's "Editor.")

which his black eyes darted here and there, he kept perfectly still. I was charmed by the sight. I sat down on a plow that stood opposite them and was greatly delighted to sketch the pose of the two brothers. I put in the nearby hedge, a barn door, and some broken wagon wheels, everything the way each stood behind the other, and after an hour I found that I had produced a well-composed, very interesting drawing without having introduced the slightest bit of myself. This strengthened me in my resolve in future to stay exclusively with nature. It alone is infinitely rich, and it alone forms the great artist. Much can be said in favor of the rules, about the same that can be said in praise of bourgeois society. A man formed by them will never produce anything vapid or in poor taste, just as someone shaped by laws and decorum can never become an unbearable neighbor or a notorious villain; on the other hand, say what you will, rules will destroy the true feeling of nature and the genuine expression thereof. You say, That is too severe! It merely supplies limits, prunes the rampant vines, etc.—Dear friend, shall I give you a parable? It is here as with love. A young heart gives itself entirely to a girl, spends every waking hour of every day with her, squanders all his energies, his entire fortune, so as to let her know at every moment that he is fully devoted to her. And then along comes a philistine, a man in public office, and says to him, My fine young man! to love is human, but you must love in a human way! Plan the hours of your day, some hours for work, and leisure hours to devote to your girl. Calculate how much money you have, and I will not say no to your giving her a present from whatever is left over from your needs but not too often, let's say for her birthday and for her name day, etc.— If the young man agrees, the result is a useful member of society, and I myself will advise any prince to give him a place on a council; except that there's an end to his love, and if he is an artist, to his art. Oh, my friends! Why does the torrent of genius gush out so rarely, so rarely come rushing in on a spring tide to shatter your amazed soul?—Dear friends, these sedate gentlemen dwell on both banks of the stream, where their little summer houses, their tulip beds and cabbage patches would be ruined, and who therefore have the sense in good time to use dams and flood channels to ward off the impending threat of danger.

MAY 27

I have, I see, fallen into raptures, parables, and declamation, and as a result I have forgotten to tell you the rest of the story of the children. Completely immersed in my painterly mood, which I described to you in yesterday's letter in a very fragmentary way, I sat on my plow for a good two hours. Then, toward evening, a young woman with a basket on her arm approaches the children, who have not stirred, and calls from a distance: Philipps, you're a very good boy.—She greeted me, I thanked her, got to my feet, came closer and asked her if she was the children's mother. She said she was, and as she gave the older boy half a roll, she lifted up the little one and kissed him with all a mother's love.—I gave the little one to my Phillips to look after, she said, and went into town with my eldest to get some white bread and sugar and an earthenware porridge bowl.—I saw those things in the basket, as its lid had fallen open.—I want to cook some soup tonight for Hans (that was the name of the youngest child); my big boy, that rascal, broke the bowl yesterday fighting with Philipps over the porridge crust.—I asked about the eldest, and she had hardly finished telling me that he was chasing a couple of geese around the meadow when he came racing up with a hazel switch for his middle brother. I chatted some more with the woman and learned that she was the schoolmaster's daughter and that her husband had gone on a trip to Switzerland to retrieve some money inherited from a relative.—They wanted to cheat him out of it, she said, and did not answer any of his letters, so he's gone there himself. If only he hasn't had an accident! I haven't heard from him.—It was hard for me to part from the woman; I gave each of the children a penny and gave her one for the youngest child too, to bring him a roll to eat with the soup the next time she went to town, and so we parted.

I tell you, my dear friend, when my mind will not rest, all my turmoil is soothed by the sight of such a creature who, calm and happy, moves through the narrow circle of her existence, making the best of things from one day to the next, watches the leaves fall, and thinks no more about it than that winter is coming.

Since that time I have often gone out there. The children are quite used to me; they get sugar when I drink coffee, and in the evening they share my bread and butter and sour milk. On Sundays they never lack for their penny, and if I'm not there after services, I've instructed the landlady to pay it out.

They confide in me, tell me this and that, and I am particularly delighted by their passions and their naïve outbursts of desire when they are with some of the other village children.

It has taken considerable effort on my part to alleviate their mother's concern that they might be inconveniencing the gentleman.

MAY 30

What I told you about painting a few days ago certainly holds true for poetry as well; all that matters is to recognize what is excellent and dare to express it, and that, of course, is saying a lot in a few words. I was present at a scene today which, perfectly copied, would make the most beautiful idyll in the world; but then, what is the sense of poetry and scenes and idylls? If we are to take pleasure in a natural phenomenon, must it always be tinkered with?

If you are expecting something lofty and refined from this introduction, you will once again be cruelly deceived; it is nothing more than a peasant boy who has inspired such lively sympathy in me.—As usual, I will tell the tale badly, and you will, as usual, I think, find that I've exaggerated; again it is Wahlheim, and always Wahlheim, that produces these rarities.

There was a party of people outside under the linden trees, drinking coffee. Because they were not quite suitable, I found some pretext to stay away.

A peasant boy came out of a neighboring house and busied himself fixing something on the plow that I sketched a few days ago. Since I liked his manner, I spoke to him and asked about his circumstances; we were soon acquainted and, as usually happens when I'm with this sort of person, were soon on familiar terms. He told me that he worked for a widow and that she treated him very well. He said so much about her and praised her so highly that I soon realized he was devoted to her, body and soul. She was no longer young, he said; she had been ill-treated by her first husband and had no wish to marry again, and his way of speaking revealed so clearly how beautiful, how alluring he found her and how fervently he wished she might choose him to wipe out the memory of her first husband's failings, that I would have to repeat his speech word for word to make you feel the pure affection, the love and devotion of this man. Yes, I would need the gifts of the greatest poet to reproduce vividly the expressiveness of his gestures, the melodiousness of his voice, the hidden fire in his glance, all at the same time. No, words cannot express the tenderness that imbued his whole being and expression; anything more I could add would only be clumsy. I was especially moved by his fear that I might form the wrong opinion about his relation to her and doubt the propriety of her conduct. How charming it was to hear him speak of her figure, her body, which had such a powerful attraction for him and captivated him even though it lacked the charms of youth—this I can reproduce only in my innermost soul. Never in my life have I seen urgent desire and hot, ardent craving in such purity: indeed I can say, a purity such as I have never conceived or dreamed of. Do not scold me if I tell you that when I remember this innocence and truth, my innermost soul glows and that the image of his loyalty and tenderness pursues me everywhere and that, as if I myself had caught its fire, I yearn and languish.

Now I must try to see her for myself as soon as possible or rather—now that I think about it—I want to avoid doing so. It is better for me to see her through the eyes of her lover; it may be that in my own eyes she would not appear as she stands before me now, and why should I spoil this beautiful image?

JUNE 16

Why haven't I written to you?—You ask, and yet you consider yourself a man of some learning? You ought to guess that I'm well, and indeed—in a word, I have made an acquaintance who has won my heart. I have—I don't know.

To tell you in an orderly fashion how I came to know one of the loveliest creatures will be a hard task. I'm full of joy and hence not a good chronicler.

An angel—bah! Everyone says that about his beloved, right? And yet I am quite unable to tell you how perfect she is and why she is perfect; it's enough to say that she has captivated all my senses.

So much simplicity together with so much understanding,

so much goodness together with such steadfastness, and calmness of soul in the midst of real life and activity.—

All I've told you about her is disgusting twaddle, tiresome abstractions that express not one single trait of her true self. Some other time—No, not some other time, I want to tell you right now. If I don't, I never will. For, just between us, since I started to write, I have three times been on the point of putting down my pen, saddling my horse, and riding out to see her. And yet I swore this morning not to ride out, and yet every minute I go to the window to see how high the sun still is.—

I could not resist, I had to go and see her. Here I am again, Wilhelm, I'll have my evening bread and butter and write to you. How my soul delights to see her amid those dear, lively children, her eight brothers and sisters!—

If I continue in this vein, you won't be any wiser at the end than you were at the beginning. So listen, I'll force myself to go into detail.

I recently wrote to you about meeting District Officer S. and how he invited me to visit him soon at his hermitage, or rather, his little kingdom. I neglected to do so, and perhaps I would never have gone had chance not disclosed the treasure that lies hidden in that quiet place.

Our young people had organized a ball in the country, which I agreed to attend. I offered to escort a local girl who is pleasant, pretty, but otherwise of little account, and it was decided that I should hire a carriage, drive out to the place where the party was to be held, along with my dance partner and her cousin, and on the way pick up Charlotte S.—You are going to meet a very pretty girl, said my companion as we drove to the hunting lodge through the wide, cleared woods.—Be careful, her cousin added, that you don't fall in love!—Why is that? I said.—She is already engaged, she replied, to a very good man, who is away on a trip. He has gone to put his affairs in order, because his father has died, and he means to apply for a good position.—The information left me quite indifferent.

The sun was still a quarter of an hour from setting behind the hills when we arrived at the courtyard gate. The air was sultry, and the women expressed their concern about a thunderstorm that seemed to be gathering at the horizon in grayish-white, sullen little clouds. I duped their fears with a pretense at meteorological expertise, although I too was beginning to suspect that our party would suffer a blow.

I got down from the carriage, and a maid who came to the gate asked us to wait a moment, Miss Lotte would be with us shortly. I walked across the yard to the handsome house, and when I had gone up the front steps and entered the doorway, I caught sight of the most charming spectacle that I have ever witnessed. In the vestibule six children from eleven to two years old crowded around a girl with a lovely figure, of medium height, wearing a simple white dress with pink ribbons on her sleeves and at her breast. She was holding a loaf of black bread and cutting off a slice for each of the little ones surrounding her, in proportion to their age and appetite, giving it to each one with such kindness, each shouting out so unaffectedly their: Thank you! after having reached up for so long with their little hands even before the slice had been cut, and now, delighted with supper, either dashing off or, if they were of a quieter nature, walking calmly toward the courtyard gate to see the strange persons and the carriage in which their Lotte was to drive off.—I beg your pardon, she said, that I made you come in and kept the ladies waiting. What with getting dressed and all sorts of instructions for the household during my absence, I forgot to give my children their supper, and they will have their bread sliced by no one else but me.—I paid her a trifling compliment, my entire soul rested on her figure, the sound of her voice, her demeanor. I just had time to recover from my surprise when she ran into the parlor to fetch her gloves and fan. Off at a distance the little ones threw me sidelong glances, and I went up to the youngest, a child with the most attractive features. He drew back just as Lotte came to the door, saying, Louis, shake hands with your cousin.— The lad did so very freely, and I could not resist giving him a heartfelt kiss despite his little runny nose.—Cousin? I said, while giving her my hand, Do you think I deserve the good fortune of being your relative?—Oh, she said, with an easy smile, our network of cousins is very extensive, and I should be sorry if you were the worst of them.—As she prepared to leave, she instructed Sophie, the next-older sister, a girl of about eleven, to keep a watchful eye on the children and to greet Papa when he returned from his ride. She told the little ones to obey their sister Sophie as if she were Lotte herself, which several of them expressly promised to do. A pert little blonde, however, about six years old, said: But you aren't her, Lotte, we like you better.—The two oldest boys had climbed up on the coach, and at my request she allowed them to ride with us to the edge of the woods as long as they promised not to tease one another and to hold on tight.

We had hardly settled in, the women greeting one another, commenting by turns on the other's outfits, especially their hats, and giving the expected guests a thorough going-over, when Lotte had the coachman stop and her brothers dismount; once again, they were eager to kiss her hand, the eldest doing just that with all the tenderness a fifteen-year-old can command, the other with much vigor and exuberance. She had them send her love to the little ones once more, and we drove on.

My partner's cousin asked whether she had finished the book she had recently sent her.—No, Lotte said, I don't care for it; you can have it back. And the one before that was no better.—I was astonished when, on asking what books they were, she replied:†——I found so strong a personality expressed in everything she said, with every word I saw new charms, new gleams of intelligence flashing from her features, which gradually appeared to blossom with delight because she sensed that I understood her.

When I was younger, she said, there was nothing I loved so much as novels. God knows how happy I was when on Sunday I could curl up in a corner and share wholeheartedly in the joys and sorrows of a Miss Jenny. Now, I won't deny that this kind of writing still holds a certain charm for me. But since I have so little time to read, it has to be something completely to my taste. And I do love best of all that author in whom I rediscover my own world, in whose books things happen the way they do all around me, and whose story is as interesting and heartfelt as my own domestic life, which, of course, is no paradise and yet all in all is a source of inexpressible happiness.

I made an effort to conceal my emotions at these words. Of course I did not get very far; for when I heard her speak in passing with such perceptiveness about *The Vicar of Wakefield* and about‡ ——,I was beside myself and said everything I had to say, and it was only after some time, when Lotte directed the conversation to the others, that I noticed that all the while they had sat there staring with wide-open eyes, as if they were not sitting there at all. My partner's cousin looked down

† We feel obliged to suppress this passage in the letter to avoid giving anyone grounds for complaint. Although at bottom it can little matter to any author what one young woman and a fickle young man think of his work. (Note by Goethe's "Editor.")
‡ Here too we have omitted the names of several German authors. Whoever shares Lotte's approval will surely feel in his heart who they are if he should read this passage, and no one else really needs to know. (Note by Goethe's "Editor.")

her nose at me more than once, but that was of no concern to me.

The conversation turned to the joy of dancing.—If this passion is a fault, said Lotte, I gladly confess to you that I know nothing better than dancing. And when something is troubling me and I drum out a country dance on my out-of-tune piano, all is well again.

How I feasted on her black eyes during this conversation! How my entire soul was drawn to her animated lips and her fresh, glowing cheeks! How completely immersed I was in the splendid sense of her conversation, so that at times I did not even hear the words with which she expressed herself!— You have some idea of this because you know me. In a word, when we came to a halt at the ballroom house, I got out of the carriage as if in a dream, and I was so lost in my dreams in the midst of the twilit world that I hardly registered the music pealing down to us from the brightly lit hall.

The two gentlemen, Audran and a certain party—who can remember all their names!—who were the cousin's and Lotte's escorts, met us at the carriage, they took charge of their ladies, and I led mine up the stairs.

We weaved around one another in minuets; I asked one lady after the other to dance, and it was precisely the most unattractive ones who could not manage to give me their hand and bring the dance to an end. Lotte and her partner began an English country dance, and you can imagine my delight when it was her turn to begin the figure with us. You should see her dance! You see, she is so absorbed in it with her heart and soul, her whole body one harmony, so carefree, so natural, as if this were the only thing in the world, as if she thought or felt nothing else; and in such moments everything else surely does vanish from her mind.

I asked her for the second country dance; she promised me the third, and with the most charming frankness in the world

assured me that she adored dancing this German variation.—
It's the custom here, she continued, that every couple that
belongs together remain together for the German dance, but
my partner waltzes badly and is grateful to me if I relieve him
of this chore. Your lady doesn't know how to and doesn't like
to, and I saw when you danced the country dance that you
waltz well; if you're willing to be my partner for the waltz, go
and ask my partner for leave, and I will speak to your lady.—I
gave her my hand upon it, and it was arranged that while we
danced, our partners would entertain one another.

So it began! and for a while we were delighted with the
various ways our arms intertwined. How charming she was,
how nimbly she moved! And now, as we began the waltz and,
like the heavenly spheres, circled around one another, there
was, of course, a good deal of confusion at first, because few
were adept. We were clever and let them exhaust themselves,
and once the clumsiest ones had left the floor, we moved in
and, together with one other couple, Audran and his partner,
carried on valiantly. Never have I danced so effortlessly. I was
no longer a mere mortal. To hold the loveliest creature in my
arms and to fly with her like the wind, so that everything else
around me vanished, and—Wilhelm, to be honest, I vowed
to myself that a girl whom I loved, to whom I was attached,
should never waltz with anyone but me, even if it were to cost
me my life. You understand what I mean!

We took a few turns around the ballroom to catch our
breath. Then she sat down, and the oranges I had set aside
and that were now the only ones left had a good effect,
though with each little segment she politely offered to a
greedy neighbor, a pang went through my heart.

At the third country dance, we were the second pair. As
we danced through the line and I, God knows with how
much bliss, hung on her arm and eyes, which were full of
the most genuine expression of the frankest, purest pleasure,

we encountered a woman whom I had noticed earlier for the gentle expression on her aging face. Smiling, she looks at Lotte, lifts a minatory finger and, as we fly past, twice utters the name Albert very meaningfully.

Who is Albert? I said to Lotte, if I may ask.—She was about to answer when we had to separate in order to move into the great figure eight, and it seemed to me that I saw signs of pensiveness on her forehead as we crossed in front of one another.—Why should I hide it from you, she said as she gave me her hand for the promenade, Albert is a fine man to whom I am as good as engaged.—Now that was not news to me (for the girls had told me on the way), and yet it was entirely new because I had not yet thought of it in connection with the woman who in so short a time had become so precious to me. Enough, I became confused, lost count, and came in between the wrong couple, so that everything went awry, and it took all of Lotte's presence of mind and tugging and pulling quickly to restore order.

The dance was not yet over when the lightning that we had long seen flashing on the horizon and that I had always pretended was only summer lightning began to grow far more pronounced and thunder drowned out the music. Three ladies broke out of the line, followed by their partners; the confusion became general, and the music stopped. It is natural, when a misfortune or something terrible takes us by surprise while we are enjoying ourselves, that the impression it makes on us is stronger than usual, partly because of the contrast, which we feel so vividly, partly, and even more, because our senses are open to perception and therefore take in an impression all the more readily. I must attribute to these causes the amazing grimaces that I saw on some of the ladies' faces. The smartest one sat in a corner, her back to the window, and covered her ears. Another knelt in front of her and hid her face in this lady's lap. A third pressed herself between them and embraced her sisters amid a thousand tears. Some wanted to go home; others, who knew even less what they were doing, lacked the presence of mind to control the impertinences of our young gourmands who seemed to be very busy snatching from the lips of those harassed beauties all the anxious prayers intended for heaven. Some of our gentlemen had gone downstairs to smoke their pipes in peace, and the rest of the company did not refuse when the landlady had the clever idea of showing us to a room with shutters and curtains. No sooner had we arrived there than Lotte busied herself arranging a circle of chairs, requesting the company to take seats, and proposing the rules of a game.

I saw several young men pursing their lips and stretching their limbs in the hope of a juicy forfeit.—We're going to play at counting, she said. Now pay attention! I am going to go around the circle from right to left, and you must count, also going around, each with the number of your turn, and that has to go like wildfire, and whoever hesitates or makes a mistake gets a slap in the face, and so on up to one thousand.—It was fun to watch. She went around the circle with an outstretched arm. One, the first began; his neighbor, two; the next one, three; and so on. Then she began to move more and more quickly. Then someone made a mistake: smack! A slap, and amid the laughter the next one too: smack! And faster and faster. I myself was hit twice, and it was with intense pleasure that I believed I noticed that these slaps were harder than the ones she handed out to the others. General laughter and commotion broke up the game before the company had counted to one thousand. Those who were most intimate drew each other aside, the thunderstorm had passed, and I followed Lotte back to the dance floor. On the way she said: The slaps made them forget the storm and everything else!— There was nothing I could say.—I was, she continued, one of those most afraid, and by pretending to be brave, so as to encourage the others, I grew brave.—We walked over to the window. Thunder rumbled in the distance, a splendid rain was falling on the land, and the most refreshing scent rose up to us in the fullness of a rush of warm air. She stood leaning on her elbows, her gaze penetrating the scene; she looked up at the sky and at me, I could see tears in her eyes, she put her hand on mine and said, Klopstock!—I immediately recalled the splendid ode that was in her thoughts, and I sank into the flood of feelings that she poured over me with this byword. I could not bear it, I bowed over her hand and kissed it as I wept the most blissful tears. And looked again into her eyes—Noble poet! If you had but seen yourself idolized in this glance—and now I never want to hear your name, so often blasphemed, ever mentioned again!

JUNE 19

I no longer remember where I stopped in my story; I do know that it was two o'clock in the morning when I went to bed and that if I had been able to harangue you with it, instead of writing, I might have kept you up until dawn.

I have not yet told you what happened on the way home from the ball, and I don't have time to tell you today either. It was the most glorious sunrise. All around us the dripping trees and the refreshed fields! The women in the party nodded off. She asked me if I would not want to join the group, no need to worry about her.—As long as I see these eyes open, I said, looking at her steadily, there's no danger of that.— And both of us held out until we reached her gate, which the maid opened quietly for her and in answer to her questions, assured her that her father and the little ones were well and still asleep. Thereupon I took leave of her with the request that I might see her again the very same day; she granted it, and I went; and since then, sun, moon, and stars can quietly go about their business, I don't know whether it's day or night, the whole world around me vanishes.

JUNE 21

I am living such happy days as God reserves for His saints; and no matter what happens to me, I cannot say that I have not tasted the joys, the purest joys of life.—You know my Wahlheim; I'm fully settled in; from here I'm only half an hour from Lotte; that is where I am in touch with myself and with all the happiness granted to man.

Had I imagined when I chose Wahlheim as the goal of my walks that it lay so close to heaven! How often on my wide wanderings have I seen the hunting lodge that now contains all my desires, either from the hillside or across the river from the meadow!

Dear Wilhelm, I have thought about this and that, about man's desire to expand, make new discoveries, roam; and then again on his inner drive to submit willingly to limitations, to carry on in the rut of habit, looking neither right nor left.

It is marvelous how I came here and gazed down from the hills into the beautiful valley, how everything all around me attracted me—The little stand of trees over there!—Oh, if you could only mingle in its shade!—There the hilltop!—Oh, if you could see over the whole wide region from up there!—The enchained hills and the gentle valleys!—Oh, if I could lose myself in them!—I hurried to be there, and returned, and had not found what I had hoped to find. Oh, distance is like the future! A vast twilit whole looms before our soul, our feeling blurs in it like our eyesight, and we long, oh, to surrender our whole being, to let ourselves be filled to the brim, blissfully, with a single, great, glorious emotion.—And alas! when we rush to be there, when there becomes here, everything is as it was before, and we stand there as poor and limited as before, and our soul craves the balm that has slipped away.

Thus, in the end, the most restless vagabond longs once more for his homeland, and in his cottage, at his wife's breast, in the circle of his children, in the occupations that provide for them, he finds the bliss that he sought in vain in the whole wide world.

When mornings at sunrise I leave for my Wahlheim, and in the garden of the inn I pick my own sugar peas, sit down, snip off their strings, and in between read my Homer; when in the little kitchen I choose a saucepan, baste the peapods with a little butter, set them on the fire, cover them, and sit there to shake the pan from time to time; then I feel vividly how Penelope's boisterous suitors slaughter, carve up, and roast oxen and swine. Nothing fills me with such serene, genuine feeling as the features of patriarchal life, which, thank God, I can weave into my way of life without affectation.

How happy I am that my heart can feel the simple, innocent bliss of the man who brings to his table the head of cabbage he has grown himself and who now, in a single moment, enjoys not only the cabbage but all the fine days, the beautiful morning he planted it, the lovely evenings he watered it, and the pleasure he took in watching it grow continuously—all rolled into one.

JUNE 29

The day before yesterday the doctor came from town to see the District Officer, and he found me on the floor with Lotte's children, several of them clambering over my back and others teasing me while I tickled them and set off a great hullabaloo. The doctor, a very dogmatic marionette who adjusts his cuffs while speaking and ceaselessly plucks at a ruffle, found my behavior beneath the dignity of a civilized man; I could see as much from his nose. But I did not let myself be bothered in the least, I let him discourse on very sensible topics, and I rebuilt the children's houses of cards whenever they knocked them down. Whereupon he went about town complaining: as if the District Officer's children weren't wild enough, Werther was now spoiling them altogether.

Yes, dear Wilhelm, the children are of all things on earth closest to my heart. When I watch them and see in these small beings the seeds of all the virtues, all the powers they will one day need so urgently; when I glimpse future steadfastness and firmness of character in their stubbornness and in their playfulness, good humor and the ease they'll need to slide over life's dangers, when I see all of it so unspoiled, so intact!—I repeat over and over again the golden words of the teacher of mankind: Unless you become as little children! and yet, dear friend, they, who are our equals, whom we ought to consider our models, these we treat as inferiors. They should not have a will of their own!—Are we then without one? And wherein does our privilege lie?—Because we are older and more intelligent!—Good God, from Your heaven You see old children and young children and nothing more; and Your son long ago proclaimed which ones give You greater joy. But they believe in Him and do not hear Him—that, too, is nothing new!—and fashion their children on their own model and— Adieu, Wilhelm! I'm not in the mood to blather on about it any longer.

JULY 1

My own poor heart, which suffers more than many who languish on their sickbeds, shows me what Lotte must mean to an invalid. She will be spending a few days in town with a good woman whose end, according to her doctors, is near and who in her final hours wants Lotte at her side. Last week I went with Lotte to visit the pastor of St. ——, a little village an hour away in the mountains. We arrived around four o'clock. Lotte had brought along her little sister. As we entered the courtyard of the parsonage, shaded by two tall walnut trees, the good old man was seated on a bench in front of the door; and when he saw Lotte, it was as if he had come to life, forgetting his knotty stick and venturing to stand up to go toward her. She ran over to him and made him sit back down by sitting beside him, bringing warm greetings from her father, and then cuddling his naughty, dirty youngest boy, the little treasure of his old age. You should have seen her keeping the old man occupied, raising her voice to make herself heard by his half-deaf ears while telling him about strapping young people who had died unexpectedly and about the excellence of Carlsbad, praising his decision to spend the next summer there, and how much better she thought he looked, much more lively than the last time she'd seen him. Meanwhile I paid my respects to the pastor's wife. The old man became quite animated, and as I could not help admiring the beautiful walnut trees that cast their shade over us so pleasantly, he began to tell us their story, although somewhat clumsily.—The old one, he said, we do not know who planted it; some say this pastor, others say a different one. But the younger tree there in the back is as old as my wife, fifty in October. Her father planted it the morning of the day she was born toward evening. He was my predecessor in office, and I can't tell you how much he loved the tree; of course, it means just as much to me. My wife was sitting under it on a log and knitting when I came into the yard for the first time as a poor student, twenty-seven years ago.—Lotte asked about his daughter: the reply was that she had gone with Herr Schmidt to the hands in the field, and the old man continued his story: how he had won the affection of his predecessor and of his daughter as well, and how he had become first his curate and then his successor. The story had barely ended when the pastor's daughter, with the aforementioned Herr Schmidt, came in through the garden; she greeted Lotte with genuine warmth, and I must say, I found her quite attractive: a vivacious, well-built brunette, who might have been quite entertaining company during a brief stay in the country. Her suitor (for Herr Schmidt immediately presented himself as such) was a refined though quiet man who would not join in our conversation, although Lotte was always quick to draw him in. What troubled me most was that I seemed to notice from his expression that it was stubbornness and ill humor more than limited intelligence that prevented him from taking part. Unfortunately, this became all too evident; for when Friederike went walking with Lotte and from time to time with me, the gentleman's face, which was swarthy to begin with, darkened so visibly that it was time for Lotte to pluck my sleeve and let me know that I had been too friendly toward Friederike. Now there is nothing that irritates me more than when people torment one another, especially when young people in the prime of life, who could be most open to all life's joys, ruin the few good days for each other with antics and realize only too late that they have squandered something irreplaceable. That nettled me, and after we had returned to the parsonage toward evening and were eating curdled milk at the table and the conversation turned to the joys and sufferings of the world, I could not help picking up the thread and speaking out very bluntly against bad moods.— People often complain, I began—for the most part unjustly, I think—that there are so few good days and so many bad ones. If our hearts were always open to enjoy the good that God puts before us each day, we would also be strong enough to endure the bad whenever it comes.—But we have no control over our feelings, replied the pastor's wife; so much depends on our bodies. When we do not feel well, nothing seems right.—I granted her that.—Well, then, I continued, let's consider moodiness as a sickness and ask if there is no cure for it.—That sounds reasonable, said Lotte: at least, I think a lot depends on ourselves. I know it does with me. If something annoys me and is apt to make me ill-tempered, I jump up and sing a few country dances up and down the garden, and it's gone right away.—That's what I meant to say, I added: bad moods are just the same as laziness, for they are a sort of laziness. Our natures are prone to it, and yet, if we just once summon up the strength to pull ourselves together, work flies from our hands, and we find real pleasure in being active.—Friederike listened very attentively, and her young man objected that we are not masters of ourselves and least of all able to dictate our feelings.—Here it is a question of an unpleasant feeling, I replied, which surely everyone would gladly be rid of; and no one knows the extent of his powers until he has tested them. Certainly, a sick man will consult all the doctors, and he will not reject the greatest deprivation, the harshest medicines, to regain the health he desires.—I noticed that the good old man was straining to take part in our conversation. I raised my voice and turned to address him. They preach sermons against so many vices, I said; I have never yet heard anyone inveighing against bad moods from the pulpit.[†]—That's a job for city pastors, he said. Peasants are not ill-humored; and yet it would do no harm now and again, as a lesson at least for my wife and for the District Officer.—We all laughed, and he laughed heartily along with us until attacked by a coughing fit, which interrupted our conversation for a while; then the young man spoke up again: You called bad moods a vice; I think that's an exaggeration.—Not at all, I replied, if whatever harms ourselves and our neighbors deserves this

† We now have an excellent sermon on this topic from Lavater, one among those on the Book of Jonah. (Note by Goethe's "Editor.")

name. Isn't it enough that we cannot make each other happy, must we also rob each other of the pleasure that every heart is still able to grant itself from time to time? And show me the man who is ill-tempered and yet is good enough to hide it, to bear it alone, without destroying the joy all around him! Isn't it rather an inner dissatisfaction with our own unworthiness, a displeasure with ourselves forever tied to envy that is stimulated by foolish vanity? We see happy people whom we are not making happy, and that is unbearable.—Lotte smiled at me as she saw the passion with which I spoke, and a tear in Friederike's eyes spurred me on.—Woe unto them, I said, who use the power they have over another's heart to rob it of the simple joys that naturally burgeon from it. All the gifts, all the favors the world can bestow cannot replace an instant of pleasure in oneself that our tyrant's envious discontent has turned to bile.

At that moment my whole heart was full; the memory of so much in the past pressed against my soul, and tears came to my eyes.

If we would only say to ourselves each day, I cried out: We can do nothing for our friends but let their joys abide and increase their happiness by enjoying it with them. When their innermost soul is tormented by an anxious passion or shattered by grief, are you able to give them a drop of comfort?

And when the final, most frightening sickness befalls the creature you undermined when she was in flower, and now she lies there in the most pitiable exhaustion, her eyes lifted insensibly toward heaven, death sweat alternating on her pallid brow, you stand before her bed like a damned soul, with the most intense feeling that with all your resources you can do nothing, and you experience an internal spasm of fear, and you would gladly give everything to be able to impart to this dying creature a drop of comfort, a spark of courage.

With these words I was overwhelmed by the memory of such

a scene at which I had been present. I put my handkerchief to
my eyes and left the party, and only Lotte's voice, which called
to me to say that it was time to leave brought me to my senses.
And how she scolded me on the way back about my excessive
emotional involvement in everything, and how that would
lead to my destruction! That I ought to spare myself!—Oh,
you angel! For your sake I must live!

JULY 6

She is always with her dying friend and is always the same,
always the fully attentive, lovely creature, who, wherever she
turns, relieves pain and makes people happy. Last night she
went for a walk with Marianne and little Amalie; I knew about
it and met them, and we walked together. After an hour and a
half we turned back toward the town and came upon the well
that is so dear to me and is now a thousand times dearer. Lotte
sat down on the low wall, and we stood in front of her. I looked
around, oh! and the time when my heart was so alone came
alive again before me.—Beloved well, I said, since that time
I have not rested beside your coolness, and sometimes, when
hurrying by, I did not even take notice of you.—I looked down
and saw that Amalie, climbing up, was fully occupied with a glass
of water.—I looked at Lotte and felt everything that she means
to me. At that moment Amalie arrived with a glass. Marianne
wanted to take it from her.—No! the child cried out with the
sweetest expression, No, dear Lotte, you must drink first! I was
so enchanted by the truth, the goodness, with which the child
cried that out that I could not express my emotion except to lift
her up and kiss her soundly, so that she began to scream and
weep at once.—You've acted badly, said Lotte.—I was struck.—
Come, Amalie, she continued, as she took her hand and led
her down the steps, wash it off in the fresh well water, hurry,
hurry, then it won't matter.—I stood there and watched with

what zeal the little girl rubbed her cheeks with her little wet hands, with what faith that this well of wonders must wash away all pollution and remove the disgrace of getting an ugly beard. I heard Lotte say: That's enough! and still the child went on eagerly washing herself as if more were better than less—I tell you, Wilhelm, I never felt greater reverence when attending a baptism; and when Lotte came back up, I would have happily thrown myself at her feet as before a prophet whose blessing had washed away the sins of a nation.

That evening the joy in my heart led me to describe the incident to a man whom I believed to have human feelings because he is intelligent; but with what results? He said that it was very wrong of Lotte; one should not fool children into believing things that are not true; that sort of thing would give rise to countless errors and superstitions, from which children must be protected at an early age.—At that point it occurred to me that the same man had had a child baptized a week before, so I let it pass and in my heart remained faithful to the truth: we ought to fare with children as God fares with us, Who makes us happiest when He lets us stumble about in our amiable delusions.

JULY 8

How childish we are! How greedy we can be for a glance! How childish we are!—We had gone to Wahlheim. The ladies drove out, and during our walks I thought I saw in Lotte's dark eyes—I am a fool, forgive me! you should see them, those eyes!—To be brief (for I am so sleepy that my eyes are closing), behold, the ladies got in, and standing around the young W.'s carriage were Selstadt, Audran, and I. The ladies chatted through the carriage door with the fellows, who of course were easy and breezy enough.—I sought Lotte's eyes: oh, her glance went from one to the other! But it did not fall on me! me! me!

the only one standing there who lives wholly in submission to her!—My heart bade her a thousand adieus! And she did not look at me! The carriage drove on, and there were tears in my eyes. I watched her go, and saw Lotte's bonnet leaning out the carriage door, and she turned around in order to look back, ah! at me?—Dear friend! I am adrift in this uncertainty; this is my comfort: perhaps she did turn around to look at me! Perhaps!—Good night! Oh, how childish I am!

JULY 10

The foolish figure I cut when I'm in company and her name is mentioned—you should see me! Especially when others ask me how I like her—*Like?* I hate this word to death. What sort of person must it be who *likes* Lotte, whose senses, whose heart she does not completely fill? *Like!* Recently someone asked me how I *liked* Ossian!

JULY 11

Frau M. is in a very bad way; I pray for her life because I share Lotte's suffering. Occasionally I see her at my friend's, a lady, and today she told me an amazing thing.—Old Herr M. is a stingy, grasping lout who during their life together kept his wife on a short leash and harassed her grievously, but she always knew how to manage. A few days ago, when the doctor told her that she did not have long to live, she sent for her husband—Lotte was in the room—and spoke to him thus: I must confess something that could cause confusion and aggravation after my death. I have always kept house as properly and thriftily as possible, but you will forgive me that for these thirty years I have gone behind your back. At the beginning of our marriage you fixed a small sum to cover the kitchen and other domestic expenses. As our household grew larger, and our business expanded, you could not be persuaded to increase my weekly allowance accordingly; in short, you know that in the times when our expenses were greatest, you insisted that I get by on seven gulden a week. I took that money without complaint, and at the end of each week I made up what was needed from the till, since no one would suspect your wife of helping herself to the receipts. I wasted nothing, and I would have been content to meet my maker without confessing, except that the woman who has to manage your household after I'm gone won't be able to do it, and you could always insist that your first wife managed to make do with her allowance.

I discussed with Lotte the unbelievable self-deception of the human mind, that a man should never suspect that something else is involved when his wife makes do with seven gulden for expenses that evidently amount to almost twice that sum. But I myself have known people who would have accepted the prophet's perpetual cruet of oil in their houses and never been surprised.

JULY 13

No, I am not deceiving myself! I read in her black eyes genuine concern for me and what may befall me! Yes, I feel, and in this I know I may trust my heart, that she—oh may I, can I express heaven in these words—that she loves me!

Loves me!—And how I begin to value myself, how I—I can certainly tell you, you understand such things—how I worship myself ever since she has come to love me!

Is this presumption or a correct sense of our real relationship?—I do not know the man whose place in Lotte's heart could make me afraid. And yet—when she speaks about her fiancé with such warmth, such love—I feel like a man deprived of all his honors and titles and stripped of his sword.

Oh, what a thrill I feel running through my veins when my finger inadvertently touches hers, when our feet meet under the table! I pull back as if from fire, and a secret force draws me forward again—all my senses grow dizzy.— Oh! and her innocence, her naïve soul does not suspect how much these little intimacies torment me. When in conversation she actually lays her hand on mine and when, to heighten our exchange, she moves closer to me so that her divine breath brushes my lips—I feel as if I'm sinking away, as if struck by lightning.—And, Wilhelm! if ever I dared . . . this heaven, this trust—! You understand me. No, my heart is not so depraved! Weak! Weak enough!—And isn't that depravity?—

She is sacred to me. All lust falls silent in her presence. I never know what I feel when I am near her; it is as if my soul ran every which way through all my nerves.—There is a tune that she plays on the piano with the touch of an angel, so simple and so soulful! It is her favorite song, she needs only to strike the first note, and I am cured of all my pain, confusion, and gloom.

No claim of the old magic power of music is implausible to me. How this simple song affects me! And she knows just when to introduce it, often at moments when I feel like putting a gun to my head! The confusion and darkness of my soul disperse, and I breathe freely again.

Wilhelm, what is the world to our heart without love! What a magic lantern is without light! No sooner have you set the little lamp inside than the most colorful pictures glow on your white screen! And if it were nothing more than that—fleeting phantoms—we are always happy when we stand before them like expectant boys and are charmed by these wondrous apparitions.

Today I could not see Lotte: an unavoidable social gathering kept me away. What was to be done? I sent my servant to her, just to have someone around me who had been near her today. How impatiently I waited for him, how joyously I welcomed him back! I would have liked to clasp his head and kiss him if I hadn't been embarrassed.

There is a story about the Bonona stone, which when placed in the sun, attracts its rays and for a while glows at night. So it was for me with this fellow. The feeling that her eyes had rested on his face, his cheeks, the buttons of his jacket, the collar of his overcoat made all of these so sacred, so valuable to me! In that moment I wouldn't have parted from him for a thousand thalers. His presence made me so happy.—God forbid that you laugh at me. Wilhelm, can these be phantoms if we feel so happy?

JULY 19

I'm going to see her! I exclaim in the morning when I wake up and with serene good cheer look out at the glorious sun; I'm going to see her! and then, for the entire day, I have no other wish. Everything, everything is consumed by this one prospect.

JULY 20

I cannot yet accept your idea that I ought to go with the ambassador to ***. I do not like being anyone's subordinate, and we all know that on top of this the man is odious. You say that my mother would like to see me actively employed; that made me laugh. Am I not now actively employed? and when you come down to it, isn't it the same whether I count peas or lentils? Everything in the world ends up as the same paltry rubbish, and anyone who works himself to the bone to please others, for money or honor or whatever else, without its being his own passion, his own necessity, is a perfect fool.

JULY 24

Since it is so important to you that I not neglect my drawing, I would much prefer to skip the whole subject than tell you how little I've been doing.

I've never been happier, my feeling for nature, right down to the smallest pebble, the smallest blade of grass, has never been more complete and more intense, and yet—I don't know how to express myself, my power of depiction is so weak, everything swims and wavers so before my soul that I cannot seize an outline; but I imagine that if I had clay or wax, I could probably shape it. I will surely take clay, if this continues, and knead it: and even if it should turn out to be mud pies!

I've begun Lotte's portrait three times, and three times I've made a mess of it. That depresses me all the more because not long ago I was very good at doing likenesses. Instead I did a silhouette of her, and that will have to do.

JULY 26

Yes, dear Lotte, I will fetch everything and order everything; only charge me with more errands, and often. I ask one thing: Stop strewing sand on the little notes you send me. Today I hastily pressed one to my lips, and my teeth crackled.

JULY 26

I've resolved more than once not to see her so often.
Yes, but who could keep to that! Every day I succumb to
temptation, and I swear a sacred promise to myself: Tomorrow
you will stay away, and when tomorrow comes, again I find
an irresistible reason, and before I know it, I am at her
house. Either the previous evening she said: You're coming
tomorrow, aren't you?—then who could stay away? Or she asks
me to run an errand, and I consider it only proper to deliver
the answer in person; or the day is simply too beautiful, I walk
to Wahlheim, and once I'm there, it's just another half-hour
to her place—I am too close to her aura—whoosh! and I'm
there. My grandmother used to tell a story about a magnetic
mountain: ships that sailed too close were suddenly stripped
of all their ironwork, the nails flew to the mountain, and
the poor wretches foundered in the crash of the collapsing
planks.

JULY 30

Albert has arrived, and I shall leave; even if he were
the best, the noblest of men, one to whom I'd be ready to
subordinate myself in every way, it would still be unbearable
to see him take possession of such perfection—Possession!—
Enough, Wilhelm, the fiancé is here! A fine, dear man, whom
one cannot help but like. Fortunately I was not present at his
arrival! It would have rent my heart. And he is so honorable
and has not kissed Lotte even once in my presence. May God
reward him for that! I have to love him for the regard he
shows her. He means well by me, and I assume that is Lotte's
doing more than his own feeling: for in this matter women
have a delicate sense, and they are right: if they can keep two

admirers on good terms with one another, they will always have the advantage, no matter how rarely that succeeds.

Meanwhile, I cannot deprive Albert of my esteem. His calm exterior stands in sharp contrast to my natural restlessness, which cannot be concealed. He is a man of feeling and knows what a treasure he has in Lotte. He appears to have few bad moods, and you know that is the sin in a person that I hate more than any other.

He considers me a person of sensibility; and my affection for Lotte, my sincere pleasure in all her actions, heightens his triumph, and he loves her all the more for it. Whether he torments her at times with little jabs of jealousy is a subject I shall not explore; at any rate, in his place I would not be wholly safe from this devil.

Be that as it may! My joy in being with Lotte is gone. Shall I call that foolishness or delusion?—Why does it need a name! The thing explains itself!—I knew everything that I now know before Albert came; I knew that I had no claim on her, nor did I make one—that is, insofar as it is possible to feel no desire in the presence of such loveliness.—And now this fool is wide-eyed with surprise when another man actually appears and takes the girl away from him.

I grit my teeth and scoff at my misery, and I would scoff doubly and triply at those who would say I ought to submit, since nothing can be done.—Get these scarecrows away from me!—I roam through the woods, and when I come to Lotte's and find Albert sitting with her under the arbor in the little garden, and I cannot go on, I become boisterously foolish and play pranks and do a lot of confused stuff.—For God's sake, Lotte said to me today, please, not another scene like the one last night! You are frightful when you're so merry.— Between you and me, I wait for the moment when he is busy with something; whoosh! I'm there, and I'm always happy when I find her alone.

AUGUST 8

I beg your pardon, dear Wilhelm, I certainly did not mean you when I called people intolerable who demand our submission to an unavoidable fate. I truly did not think that you could be of a similar mind. And basically you're right. Only one thing, my good friend: In this world it is seldom a matter of either-or; feelings and actions display as many shadings as the gradations between a hawk nose and a turned-up one.

And so you won't be offended if I concede your entire argument and still search for a way to slip in between the either and the or.

Either, you say, you have hopes of winning Lotte, or you have none. Fine, in the first case, try to bring them to a conclusion, try to seize the fulfillment of your wishes: in the other case, be a man and try to rid yourself of a miserable passion that must consume all your powers.—My dear friend! That is well said—and easily said.

And can you require of the unfortunate man whose life is inexorably ebbing away by degrees from an insidious disease, can you require of him that he put an end to his torment once and for all with the thrust of a dagger? And does not the disease that is consuming his strength at the same time rob him of the courage to free himself?

Of course you could answer with a similar analogy: Who would not rather cut off his arm than risk his life through dallying and delay?—I don't know!—And we don't want to nip at each other with analogies. Enough.—Yes, Wilhelm, there are moments when I feel a fit of the courage to spring up and shake it all off and then—if only I knew where to, I think I would go.

EVENING

My diary, which I have neglected for some time, fell into my hands again today, and I am amazed at how knowingly I went into all this, step by step! How I have always seen my situation so clearly and yet have acted like a child; even now I see it so clearly, and still there is no sign of improvement.

AUGUST 10

I could be leading the best, the happiest life if I weren't a fool. Wonderful circumstances such as those in which I now find myself do not easily come together to delight a man's soul. Oh, it is so certain that it is our heart alone that makes for happiness.—To be a member of the charming family, to be loved by her father as a son, by the little ones as a father, and by Lotte!—then the honorable Albert, who never disturbs my happiness with moody behavior; who accepts me with sincere friendship; for whom, next to Lotte, I am the dearest person in the world.—Wilhelm, it is a joy to hear us when we go for a walk, speaking to one another of Lotte: nothing in the world has been invented that is more ridiculous than this relationship, and yet it often brings tears to my eyes when he tells me about her honest, virtuous mother: how on her deathbed she handed her house and her children over to Lotte and gave Lotte into his care; and how since that time a quite different spirit has inspired Lotte, how she, in her concern for the household and in her seriousness, had become a true mother, how not a moment of her time passes without active love, without work, and yet despite this, her good cheer, her blitheness have never left her.—I walk along beside him and pluck flowers by the roadside, piece them very carefully into a bouquet and—toss them into the stream that flows by and gaze after them as the current carries them gently downstream.—I don't know whether I've written to you that Albert will remain here and will receive a position with a nice income from the Court, where he is very well liked. I have rarely seen his equal for orderly and diligent competence in business.

AUGUST 12

Surely Albert is the best man in all creation. Yesterday the two of us had a remarkable scene. I went to say good-bye to him, for I was overcome by the desire to ride into the mountains, whence I'm now writing to you; and while pacing up and down in his room, I caught sight of his pistols.—Lend me the pistols, I said, for my trip.—As you like, he said, if you will take the trouble of loading them; in my house they hang only for show.—I took one down, and he continued: Ever since my caution played such a nasty trick on me, I don't want to have anything more to do with them.—I was curious to know the story—For some three months, he began, I was staying with a friend in the country, had a brace of unloaded small pistols, and slept peacefully. One rainy afternoon, I was sitting around idly, and it occurred to me, I don't know why, that we could be attacked, we could have need of the pistols and could—you know how it is.—I gave them to a servant to clean and load; and he fooled around with the maids, meant to frighten them, and God knows how, the weapon went off, and since the ramrod was still lodged in the barrel, he shot the ramrod into the ball of one of the girls' right hand and shattered her thumb. Then there was her wailing to be put up with, and besides, I had to pay for the treatment, and since that time I keep all weapons unloaded. Oh my dear fellow, what is caution? When it comes to danger, you live and learn!

True, but—Now you know that I am very fond of the man, up until his *True, but;* for isn't it self-evident that every general statement admits of exceptions? But the man is so eager to justify himself! When he thinks he's said something in haste, a generality, a half-truth, he won't stop limiting, modifying, and adding on and taking back, until finally there's nothing left of the statement. And on this occasion he became deeply enmeshed in his subject: I finally stopped listening altogether, fell into a black mood, and with an abrupt gesture pressed the mouth of the pistol to my forehead over my right eye.— Ugh! said Albert and took the pistol from me, What is that supposed to mean?—It's not loaded, I said.—Even so, what is that? he replied impatiently. I cannot imagine that a man can be so foolish as to shoot himself; the mere thought fills me with revulsion.

Why is it that you people, I exclaimed, whenever you speak about anything, immediately find yourself saying: this is foolish, this is clever, this is good, this is bad! And what is that supposed to mean? Have you investigated the deeper circumstances of an action to that end? Are you able to explain the causes definitively, why it happened, why it had to happen? If you had done so, you would not be so hasty with your judgments.

You will grant me, said Albert, that certain actions are vicious however they occur, whatever motives are adduced.

I shrugged and conceded the point.—Still, my dear fellow, I continued, here, too, there are some exceptions. It is true, stealing is a vice; but the man who sets out to steal to save himself and his family from imminent starvation: does he deserve pity or punishment? Who will cast the first stone against the husband who, in righteous anger, makes short shrift of his unfaithful wife and her worthless seducer? Against the girl who, in an hour of ecstasy, gives herself over to the irresistible joys of love? Even our laws, these cold-blooded pedants, can be moved to withhold their punishment.

That is something completely different, replied Albert, because a man swept away by passion loses all his powers of reason and is viewed as a drunkard or a madman.

Oh, you rationalists! I exclaimed, smiling. Passion! Drunkenness! Madness! You stand there, so calmly, without any understanding, you moral men! You chide the drinker, despise the man bereft of his senses, pass by like the priest, thank God like the Pharisee that He did not make you as one of these. I have been drunk more than once, my passions were never far from madness, and I regret neither: for in my own measure I have learned to grasp how all extraordinary men who have achieved something great, something seemingly impossible, have inevitably been derided as drunkards or madmen.

But even in ordinary life it is intolerable to hear what is shouted after almost everyone who has committed a halfway free, noble, unanticipated deed: the man is drunk, he's crazy! Shame on you, you men of sobriety! Shame on you, you wise men!

Those are some more of your quirky notions, said Albert, you exaggerate everything, and in this case, at least, you are quite wrong when you compare suicide, which is the subject under discussion, with great deeds: since it cannot be regarded as anything but a weakness. There can be no question that it is easier to die than to endure steadfastly a life of torment.

I was about to break off; for no argument makes me lose my composure more quickly than the introduction of some vacuous commonplace when I am speaking from the bottom of my heart. But I pulled myself together, because I had often heard it and had more often become angry on hearing it, and I responded with some vehemence: You call that weakness? I beg of you, don't be misled by appearances.

A people groaning under the unbearable yoke of a tyrant, do you call them weak when they finally rise up and break their chains? A man who, terror-stricken when he sees his house on fire, feels all his strength at its peak and easily carries away loads that he can barely move when he is composed; someone who, infuriated by an insult, attacks six men and overpowers them—should these men be called weak? And, my good man, if exertion is strength, why should extreme exertion be the reverse?—Albert looked at me and said: No offense, but the examples you give seem not at all relevant.—That may be, I said, I have often been criticized for combining ideas sometimes to the point of blathering. So let us see whether we can find a different way to imagine the state of mind of the man who decides to cast off what is normally the pleasant burden of life. After all, only to the degree that we sympathize do we have the right to speak about a subject. Human nature, I continued, has its limits: it can endure joy, sorrow, pain up to a certain degree, and it perishes the minute *it* is exceeded. Here, then, the question is not whether one is weak or strong but rather whether one can endure the measure of one's suffering—be it moral or physical; and I find it just as odd to say that the man who takes his own life is a coward as it would be improper to call the man who dies from a malignant fever a coward. Paradoxical! Very paradoxical! exclaimed Albert.— Not so much as you think, I replied. Grant me this: we call it a sickness unto death when human nature is so assaulted that its forces are partly consumed, partly so lamed that it is no longer able to recover, through no fortunate turn of events able to restore the normal circulation of life.

Now, my dear friend, let us apply that to the mind. Look at a man within his limitations, the way impressions affect him, ideas become entrenched in him, until finally a growing passion robs him of all his powers of calm reflection and destroys him.

It is futile for the composed, rational man to appraise the condition of the unhappy person, futile to cheer him up! Just as a healthy man who stands at the bed of a sick person cannot impart to him the least part of his powers.

For Albert that was all too general. I reminded him of a girl who had recently been found in the water, dead, and repeated her story to him.—A young thing, who grew up in the narrow circle of domestic occupations, specific weekly chores, who knew no further prospect of pleasure than, say, strolling through town of a Sunday with girls like her, in a pretty outfit pieced together over time, perhaps going to dances on all the major holidays, and for the rest chatting away her spare hours with a neighbor with all the liveliness of genuine participation about the cause of a quarrel or about some calumny, and now her fiery nature has finally come to feel more burning needs, which are heightened by the flatteries of men; bit by bit her former pleasures become distasteful, until finally she meets a man to whom she is irresistibly drawn by a strange new feeling, and now she puts all her hopes in him, forgets the world around her, hears nothing, sees nothing, feels nothing but him, her one and only, longs only for him, her one and only. Unspoiled by the vapid pleasures of a fickle vanity, her desire moves directly toward its goal, she wants to become his, bound to him for all eternity, she wants to encounter all the happiness she lacks, enjoy the union of all the joys she longs for. A repeated promise that seals the certainty of all her hopes, bold caresses that increase her desires, wholly captivate her soul; she hovers in a muffled awareness, a premonition of all the joys, she is in a state of extreme tension, finally she stretches out her arms to embrace all her desires—and her lover abandons her.—Paralyzed, out of her senses, she stands before an abyss; darkness is all around her, no prospect, no consolation, no intimation of a future! for he has abandoned her, the man in whom alone she felt her being. She does not see the great world that lies before her, the many men who could make up her loss, she feels herself alone, abandoned by the whole world—and blindly, cornered by the terrible need of her heart, she plunges down to stifle all her pains in the death that envelops her all around.—Look, Albert; that is the story of so many people! and tell me, isn't it the same with sickness? Nature finds no way out of the maze of these tangled and conflicting forces, and the man or woman must die.

Woe to him who can look on and say: Foolish girl! Had she only waited, had let time work its wonders, her despair would have subsided, another would certainly have come forward to comfort her.—That's the same as if someone were to say: The fool, dies of a fever! Had he waited until his strength had returned, his humors improved, the tumult of his blood calmed down: everything would have been well, and he would be alive to this day!

Albert, who was still not persuaded by the comparison, made a few further objections, among them this one: I had spoken only of an ignorant girl; but how an intelligent man, who was not so limited, who commanded a wide view of many relationships, might be excused was something he could not conceive.—My friend, I exclaimed, a man is a man, and the modicum of reason he might have counts for little or nothing when passion rages and the limits of human being press against him! Rather—Another time for that, I said, and reached for my hat. Oh, my heart was so full—and we parted without having understood one another. As in this world no one readily understands the other.

AUGUST 15

There is no doubt that in this world nothing but love makes another person indispensable. I can tell from Lotte that she would not like to lose me, and the children have no other idea than that I'll be back the following day. I went today to tune Lotte's piano, but I could not get to it because the children pestered me to tell them a story, and Lotte herself said that I should do what they wanted. I sliced their bread for supper, which they now accept almost as gladly from me as from Lotte, and told them my favorite story of the princess whose servants were hands. I learn a lot from this, I assure you, and I am amazed at the impression it makes on them. There are times when I have to invent some crucial detail, which by the second telling I've forgotten, and then they immediately say, it was different last time, so that now I practice reciting to them like clockwork, with an unvarying singsong intonation. From this I've learned how an author will inevitably do harm to his book in a second, revised version of his story, even though it may now be so much better poetically. The first impression finds us willing, and man is so constituted that he can be persuaded of the most outlandish things; but these details also attach themselves firmly, and woe to him who now wants to scrap them and extirpate them.

AUGUST 18

Does it have to be this way, that whatever it is that makes a man blissfully happy in turn becomes the source of his misery?

The full, warm feeling of my heart for living nature, which flooded me with such joy, which turned the world around me into a paradise, has now become an unbearable torturer, a tormenting spirit that pursues me wherever I turn. When, looking out from these rocks across the river to those hills, I used to survey the fruitful valley and was aware of the sprouting and swelling of all that surrounded me; when I saw those hills clothed from foot to peak with tall, closely ranked trees, saw those valleys with their many turnings shaded by the loveliest woods and the gentle stream gliding between the lisping reeds and mirroring the lovely clouds that the gentle evening winds rocked, as in a cradle, across the sky; when I heard the birds around me lend life to the forest while a million swarms of gnats boldly danced in the last red rays of the sun, whose final quivering glance roused the humming beetle from the grass, and the whirring and weaving around me made me look to the ground and to the moss that wrests its nourishment from these hard rocks, and the shrubbery that grows along the barren sand dunes revealed to me the innermost glowing sacred life of nature: how my warm heart enfolded all that, how I felt like a god among the overflowing abundance, and the glorious shapes of the infinite world entered and quickened my soul. Enormous mountains surrounded me, chasms lay before me, and swollen brooks plunged downward, streams rushed beneath me, and woods and mountains resounded; and I saw them, all the unfathomable forces, entwined in their hustle and bustle in the depths of the earth; and now, above the earth and under the skies swarm all the species of the manifold creatures, and everything, everything is populated with a thousand shapes; and then men shelter together in their little houses and build their nests and think they govern the whole wide world! Poor fool, who thinks so little of everything because you are so little.—From the inaccessible mountains across the deserts where no one has set foot, to the ends of the unexplored oceans wafts the spirit of the eternally creative One, delighting in every speck of dust that senses it and lives.—Oh, then, how often did I long to have the wings of the crane soaring above me to fly to the shores of the uncharted oceans, to drink that surging joy of life from the foaming beaker of infinity, and to feel for even a moment in the confined power of my breast a drop of the bliss of that Being that brings forth everything in and through Itself.

My brother, the very memory of those hours makes me glad. Even the effort of summoning up and expressing once again those ineffable feelings lifts my soul and makes me feel twice over the fear of the condition that now enfolds me.

It is as if a curtain had been drawn back from my soul, and the spectacle of infinite life is transformed before my eyes into the abyss of an ever-open grave. Can you say: This is what is! since everything passes, since everything rolls on with the swiftness of a passing storm, so rarely does the entire force of its existence last, oh! torn along into the river and submerged and shattered on the rocks? There is no moment that does not consume you and those near and dear to you, no moment when you are not a destroyer, must be one; the most innocent stroll costs the lives of thousands and thousands of tiny creatures; one footstep shatters the laboriously erected structures of the ant and pounds a tiny world into a miserable grave. Ha! I am not moved by the great, rare disasters of this world, those floods that wash away your villages, those earthquakes that swallow your cities; my heart is undermined by the destructive force that is concealed in the totality of nature; which has never created a thing that has not destroyed its neighbor or itself. And so I stagger about in fear! heaven and earth and their interweaving forces around me: I see nothing but an eternally devouring, eternally regurgitating monster.

AUGUST 21

In vain I stretch out my arms to her in the morning when I wake dazed from oppressive dreams, in vain I seek her in the night in my bed when a happy, innocent dream has deceived me into thinking that I am sitting beside her on the meadow, holding her hand, and covering it with a thousand kisses. Oh, when then, half dizzy with sleep, I grope my way toward her and wake myself—a river of tears breaks from my anxious heart, and disconsolate, I weep as I face a dark and gloomy future.

AUGUST 22

It is a catastrophe, Wilhelm, my powers of action have been jangled into a restless indolence; I cannot be idle, and yet I cannot do anything either. I have no power of imagination, no feeling for nature, and books repel me. When we are inadequate in ourselves, everything seems inadequate to us. I swear to you, sometimes I wish I were a day laborer, if only on waking in the morning I could have a clear view of the day to come, a striving, a hope. Often I envy Albert, whom I see up to his ears in screeds, and I imagine how content I'd be in his place! More than once I've been tempted to write to you and the minister to apply for the position with the embassy, which, as you assure me, I would not be refused. I myself believe that to be true. The minister has been fond of me for a long time, and for a long time he has urged me to devote myself to some occupation or other; and for an hour at a time I'm inclined to do so. But then, when I think it over and am reminded of the fable of the horse that, having grown impatient of its freedom, asks to be saddled and harnessed and is ridden until it falls—I don't know what I ought to do.—And, my dear friend! isn't my longing for a change of condition an inner, discontented impatience that will follow me wherever I go?

AUGUST 28

It's true, if my sickness could be cured, these people would cure it. Today is my birthday, and early in the morning I received a little package from Albert. When I opened it, I immediately caught sight of one of the pink ribbons that Lotte

71

wore the first time I saw her and for which I had asked her several times since. There were two small volumes in duodecimo, the little Wetstein Homer, an edition that I'd so often longed for, so that I would not have to drag the Ernesti volume on my walks. You see! This is how they anticipate my wishes, this is how they contrive all the little favors of friendship that are a thousand times more valuable than those dazzling gifts that serve only to crush us with the giver's vanity. I kiss this ribbon a thousand times, and with every breath I draw I drink in the memory of the bliss with which those few, happy, irretrievable days glutted me. Wilhelm, this is how things are, and I'm not complaining: the flowers of life are only fleeting apparitions! How many fade without leaving a trace behind, how few bear fruit, and how few of these fruits ripen! And yet enough remain; and yet—Oh, my brother!—can we neglect ripened fruit, spurn it, allow it to rot unenjoyed?

Farewell! It is a glorious summer; I often sit in the fruit trees in Lotte's orchard with the long, spiked pole, and fetch the pears from the treetop. She stands below and takes them when I hand them down to her.

AUGUST 30

Wretched creature! Are you not a fool? Aren't you deluding yourself? What is the meaning of this raging, endless passion? I have no prayers other than those directed to her; no shape appears to my imagination other than hers, and I see everything in the world around me only in relation to her. And that gives me many happy hours—until I must once again tear myself away from her! Oh Wilhelm! the things my heart often urges me to do!—When I have sat beside her for two or three hours and feasted on her figure, her demeanor, the heavenly expression of her words, and all my senses are gradually stretched to the breaking point, when it grows dark

before my eyes, when I can hardly hear and my throat feels seized by an assassin, then my wildly beating heart seeks to release my plagued senses and only increases their confusion—Wilhelm, often I do not know whether I belong to this world! And—except when, from time to time, melancholy gets the better of me and Lotte allows me the miserable solace of weeping tears of anguish over her hand—then I must leave, must go away! and then I roam far and wide over the fields; then my joy lies in climbing a steep mountain, hacking a path through an impassable forest, through hedges that hurt me, through thorns that tear at me! Then I feel a little better! A little! And when, on my way, I sometimes lie down from weariness and thirst, sometimes in the deep of night, when the full moon stands high above me, I sit on a gnarled tree in the lonely forest so as to give my torn soles some relief and then fall into a slumber in an exhausted calm at the first glow of dawn! Oh Wilhelm! the lonely dwelling of a cell, the hair shirt, and a girdle of thorns would be the balm for which my soul languishes. Adieu! I see no end to this misery except the grave.

SEPTEMBER 3

I must go away! I thank you, Wilhelm, for making my wavering decision definite. For two weeks now I have harbored the thought of leaving her. I must go away. She is in town again, visiting a friend, a lady. And Albert—and—I must go away!

SEPTEMBER 10

What a night that was! Wilhelm! Now I can live through anything. I shall never see her again! Oh, that I cannot throw my arms around your neck and with a thousand tears and ecstasies, my dear friend, express the feelings that assail my heart. Here I sit, gasp for breath, try to calm myself, wait for morning, and the horses have been ordered for dawn.

Ah, she is sleeping peacefully and has no idea that she will never see me again. I have torn myself away, and I was strong enough not to betray my intentions during a conversation that lasted two hours. And, good God, what a conversation!

Albert had promised to be in the garden with Lotte immediately after the evening meal. I stood on the terrace under the tall chestnut trees and kept my eyes on the sun, which was now setting for me for the last time over the lovely valley, over the gentle stream. How many times had I stood here with her, watching the same glorious spectacle, and now—I paced back and forth along the avenue of trees that was so dear to me; a secret sympathy had so often held me here, even before I knew Lotte, and how happy we were when, at the beginning of our acquaintance, we discovered our shared affection for this spot, which truly is one of the most romantic I have ever seen produced in art.

First, you have the distant prospect between the chestnut trees—Ah, I remember, I have already written you, I think, a lot about it, how high walls of beeches finally enclose you, and how an abutting grove makes the avenue ever darker, until finally everything ends in an enclosed small spot around which hover all the thrills of solitude. I still feel the sense of secrecy I experienced when I entered for the first time one day at high noon; I dimly felt what a stage that could become for bliss and for pain.

For about half an hour I had been savoring the devastating, sweet thoughts of parting, of meeting again, when I heard them coming up to the terrace. I ran to meet them, and with a chill I took her hand and kissed it. We had just arrived at the top when the moon rose behind the bush-covered hill; we spoke of many things, and without being aware of it, we approached the dark little garden house. Lotte entered and sat down, Albert beside her, and I as well; but my restlessness did not let me sit for long; I stood, went over to her, paced back and forth, sat down again: I was in an anxious state. She called our attention to the fine effect of the moonlight, which at the end of the high walls of beech trees lit up the entire terrace before us: a glorious sight, all the more striking because deep dusk encircled us. We were quiet, and after a while she began: I never walk in the moonlight, never, without being reminded of those dear to me who have died, without being overcome by the feeling of death, of what's to come. We shall be! she continued in a voice full of the most glorious feeling; but, Werther, shall we find one another again? Know one another again? What do you feel? What do you say?

Lotte, I said, as I took her hand in mine and as my eyes filled with tears, we shall see each other again! Here and there we shall see each other again!—I could not continue— Wilhelm, did she have to ask me that just when my heart was full of this fearful departure! And if the dear departed know about us, she continued, if they sense, when all is well with us, that we think of them with warm love? Oh! The figure of my mother forever hovers nearby when I sit in the quiet of an evening amid her children, amid my children, and they are gathered around me as they were gathered around her. Then, when I look heavenward with a tear of longing and wish that she could look in on us for a moment and see how I keep the promise I made her at the hour of her death: to be the mother of her children. With what emotion I exclaim: Forgive me, dearest, if I am not to them what you were to them. Ah! I do everything I can; they are clothed, fed, and, ah, what is more, cared for and loved. If you could see the harmony between us, dear saint! with the most ardent thanks you would glorify God whom you asked for the welfare of your children with your last, most bitter tears.

She said that! Oh, Wilhelm, who can repeat what she

said! How can the cold, dead letter represent this divine blossoming of the spirit! Albert gently interrupted her: This affects you too strongly, dear Lotte! I know that your soul is deeply attached to these ideas, but I beg of you.—Oh, Albert, she said, I know you haven't forgotten the evenings when all of us sat at the little round table when Papa was traveling and we had put the little ones to bed. Often you had a good book, and you so rarely got to read anything—wasn't the company of this glorious soul greater than anything else? This beautiful, gentle, cheerful woman, always busy! God knows the tears with which I so often threw myself on the bed before Him: that He make me be like her.

Lotte! I cried, as I threw myself before her, took her hand, and moistened it with a thousand tears, Lotte! God's blessing rests upon you, and so does your mother's spirit!—If you had known her, she said, as she squeezed my hand—she was worth your knowing her!—I thought I would faint. Never before had a grander, prouder sentence been uttered about me— and she continued: and this woman had to die in her prime, when her youngest son was not yet six months old! Her illness was not a long one; she was quiet, resigned, in pain only for her children, especially the little one. As the end approached, she said to me: Bring them to me, and I brought them in, the little ones, who did not understand, and the older ones, who were beside themselves, how they stood around her bed, and how she lifted her hands and prayed over them and she kissed them one by one and she sent them away and said to me: Be their mother!—I gave her my hand as a pledge.—You promise a lot, my daughter, she said, a mother's heart and a mother's eye. I have often seen by your tears of gratitude that you feel what these things mean. Have them for your brothers and sisters, and for your father have the loyalty and obedience of a wife. You will comfort him.—She asked for him, he had gone out to conceal from us the unbearable grief that he felt, the man was utterly broken.

Albert, you were in the room. She heard footsteps and inquired and asked that you come to her, and how she looked at you and me, with her comforted, calm gaze, seeing that we were happy, would be happy together.—Albert threw his arms around her neck and kissed her and cried: We are! We shall be!—Albert, the calm one, had completely lost his composure, and I was no longer conscious of myself.

Werther, she began, that this woman should have passed away! God! when I think sometimes how we allow the loveliest thing in life to be carried off, and no one feels that so keenly as the children, who went on bewailing that the Black Men had carried Mama off.

She stood, and I was aroused and shaken, remained seated, and held her hand.—We should leave, she said, it's time.—She wanted to pull her hand back, and I grasped it more tightly.—We will meet again, I cried, we will find each other, we will know each other among all the shapes. I'm going, I continued, I go willingly, and yet, although I should have said forever, I could not bear it. Farewell, Lotte! Farewell, Albert! We will meet again.—Tomorrow, I think, she replied jokingly.—I felt that tomorrow! Oh, she did not know, when she took her hand from mine.—They went out along the tree-lined avenue, I stood, gazed after them in the moonlight, and threw myself on the ground and wept and wept and jumped up and ran out onto the terrace and still saw below in the shadow of the tall linden trees her white dress shimmering at the garden door, I stretched out my arms, and it vanished.

~ BOOK TWO ~

OCTOBER 20, 1771

WE ARRIVED yesterday. The ambassador is indisposed and so will keep to his quarters for several days. If he weren't so disagreeable, everything would be well. I see, I see that fate has some hard tests in store for me. But be of good cheer! A light heart can put up with anything! A light heart? It makes me laugh, the way this word slips from my pen. Oh, a touch more lightheartedness would make me the happiest man under the sun. What! There, where others, with their bit of vigor and talent, swagger around before me, complacent and self-satisfied—there, am I to doubt my vigor, my gifts? Dear God, Who endows me with all I have, why didn't You withhold

79

half and give me self-confidence and contentment? Patience!
Patience! It will get better. Because I tell you, dear friend,
you're right. Ever since I've been knocking around every day
among these people and see what they do and how they go
about it, I hold myself in much higher regard. Certainly, since
we are so constituted as to compare everything with ourselves
and ourselves with everything, our happiness or misery lies
in the objects with which we are associated, and so there's
nothing more dangerous than solitude. Our imagination,
urged by its nature to elevate itself, nourished by the
visionary images of poetry, conjures up a series of beings of
whom we are the meanest, and everything outside ourselves
seems more splendid, everyone else more accomplished. And
that happens quite naturally. So often we feel that we lack
so much, and precisely what we lack often seems to us to be
possessed by someone else, to whom we then also attribute
everything that *we* possess, and on top of that a certain
idealized contentment. In this way, this fortunate person is
completely perfect, the creature of our own making.

On the other hand, if with all our weakness and effort
we simply continue to work, we often find that, with all our
delaying and tacking, we make better headway than others do
with their sailing and rowing—and—it is indeed a true sense
of self to keep up with others or actually run ahead of them.

NOVEMBER 26

I'm beginning to feel reasonably well here, as far as that
goes. The best part of it is that there is enough to do; and then
the variety of people, all sorts of new figures, stage a colorful
spectacle for my soul. I have met Count C., a man I cannot
help but admire more and more each day, a broad-minded,
powerful intellect who, even though he has so comprehensive
a view, is not coldhearted; whose company radiates so much

capacity for friendship and love. He took a well-meaning interest in me when I was sent to him on some business, and at our first words he realized that we understood one another, that he could speak with me as he could not speak with everyone. Nor can I praise his frank behavior toward me highly enough. There is no joy in the world so true or heartwarming as seeing a great soul opening itself to one.

DECEMBER 24

The ambassador is causing me a great deal of annoyance, I saw it coming. He is the most exacting fool in the world; one step at a time and as fussy as a maiden aunt; a man who is never satisfied with himself and whom, therefore, it is impossible to please. I like to work quickly, and however it comes out, that's how it stands; but then he's capable of returning a document to me and saying—It's good, but go over it again, you can always find a better word, a nicer expression.—That raises my hackles. Not a single "and" or any other little conjunction may be omitted, and he is a mortal enemy of the inverted word order that sometimes escapes me; if you don't crank out a complex sentence according to the traditional melody, he understands nothing of what's in it. It is agony to have to deal with such a man.

Count C.'s confidence is still the one thing that makes up for it. The other day he told me quite frankly how dissatisfied he is with the ambassador's slowness and pettifoggery. Such persons make life difficult for themselves and others; and yet, he said, one must resign oneself to it like the traveler who must climb over a mountain; of course, if the mountain were not there, the road would be much easier and shorter; but in the last resort it is there, and one must get over it!—

The old man certainly senses the Count's preference for me over him; this annoys him, and he seizes every opportunity

THE SUFFERINGS OF YOUNG WERTHER

to say mean things about the Count to me. I contradict him, of course, only making matters worse. Yesterday he really vexed me with a remark that was aimed at me as well: The Count was quite good at worldly affairs, such work comes easily to him, and he writes well, but like all dilettantes, he lacks genuine erudition. With this he made a face as much as to say: Did you feel the thrust? But it did not have the desired effect on me; I despise a man who can think and behave like that. I held my own and fought back quite vehemently. I said the Count was a man whom one had to respect for his character as well as his knowledge. I have not known anyone, I said, who had succeeded so well in enlarging his mind and extending it over countless subjects and yet keeping an aptitude for ordinary life.—This was all Greek to his small brain, and I took my leave so as not to choke on even more gall over such nonsense.

And it is all your fault—you people who talked me into this yoke and made such a song and dance about being active. Activity! If the man who plants potatoes and rides to town to sell his grain doesn't do more than I do, I'll spend another ten years slaving away in the galleys to which I am now shackled.

And the perfect misery, the boredom among these vile people on view here, cheek by jowl! Their thirst for rank, how they are ever on the alert, looking to gain the advantage of one tiny step ahead of the other; the most miserable, pitiable passions, all nakedly on display. There is a woman, for example, who tells everyone about her noble rank and her country, so that every stranger must think: What a fool, who considers herself wonderful for her little bit of nobility and the importance of her country.—But it is much worse: this same woman is from around here, the daughter of a local magistrate's clerk.—You see, I can't comprehend a breed of humanity that has so little sense as to disgrace itself so stupidly.

Of course, dear friend, I do notice more and more every day how foolish it is to judge others by oneself. And because I am so preoccupied with myself and this heart of mine is so stormy—alas, I'll gladly let the others go their own way, if only they would let me go mine.

What irritates me most are the disastrous social conditions. Of course, I know as well as anyone how necessary class distinctions are, how many advantages I myself derive from them: but they should not stand in my way just where I might still savor a little joy, a glimmer of happiness on earth. Recently, on a walk, I met a Fräulein von B., an adorable creature who has retained a great deal of naturalness in the midst of this rigid life. We were both pleased with our conversation, and as we were parting, I asked for permission to call on her. She agreed so straightforwardly that I could hardly wait for a suitable moment to pay my visit. She is not from here and lives with an aunt. I did not like the expression on the old woman's face. I was very attentive to her, my remarks were mainly addressed to her, and in less than half an hour I had essentially figured out what the young lady herself confessed to me subsequently: that in her old age her dear aunt lacked everything, had no respectable income, no intellect, and no support other than her ancestry, no security other than the social class in which she barricaded herself, and no pleasure other than looking down from her upper landing over the heads of the bourgeoisie. She is supposed to have been beautiful in her youth but squandered her life, first by tormenting many a poor fellow with her whims, and in her more mature years by bowing down obediently to an elderly officer, who for such a reward and a passable income spent his bronze age with her and died. Now in her iron age she finds herself alone and would not even be noticed if her niece were not so agreeable.

JANUARY 8, 1772

What sort of people are these, whose whole soul rests on ceremony, whose thoughts and struggles are bent on shoving themselves year after year one seat higher up at the table! And it is not as if they had nothing else to do: no, on the contrary, work piles up precisely because petty annoyances prevent them from attending to important matters. Last week there were quarrels during the sleigh ride, and all the fun was ruined.

Those fools, who do not see that it is not the position that matters and that the person who has the top position so rarely plays the top role! How many kings are ruled by their ministers, how many ministers by their secretaries! And who, then, is first? The one, it seems to me, who can see through the others and who has enough power or cunning to harness their strengths and passions to the execution of his plans.

JANUARY 20

I must write to you, dear Lotte, here in the taproom of a lowly peasant tavern, where I've taken refuge from a heavy storm. For as long as I roamed around the dreary hick town of D——, among strangers, people who are entirely strangers to my heart, I have not had a moment, not one, in which my heart urged me to write to you; and now, in this hovel, in this solitude, in this confinement, with snow and hailstones beating against the windowpane, here you were my first thought. As I came in, I was overcome with your image, the memory of you, oh Lotte! so sacred, so warm! Good God! The first happy moment once again.

If you could see me, my dearest, in this tumult of distractions! How parched my senses are becoming! Not One moment of fullness of the heart, not One blessed hour!

nothing! nothing! I stand as if in front of a peep show and see the manikins and tiny horses jerk around in front of me, and I often ask myself whether it is not an optical illusion. I play along, or rather, I am played like a marionette, and sometimes I take my neighbor's wooden hand and shrink back with a shudder. At night I resolve to enjoy the sunrise, and I do not get out of bed; during the day I hope to enjoy the moonlight, and I stay in my room. I do not really know why I get up and why I go to bed.

The leaven that used to set my life in motion is missing; the charm that kept my spirits up in the depths of the night, that woke me from my sleep in the morning is gone.

Here I've found a single female being, a Fräulein von B., she is like you, dear Lotte, if anyone can be like you. Oh my! you'll say, the fellow is resorting to pretty compliments! That's not entirely untrue. For some time I have been very gallant because I cannot be anything else, I'm very witty, and the ladies say: No one could ever hand out praise as elegantly as I (or tell lies, they add, for without doing so, it cannot be done, don't you agree?). But I wanted to talk about Fräulein B. She has a great soul, which shines out from her blue eyes. Her social class is a burden to her, one that gratifies none of her heart's desires. She longs to be away from the hubbub, and for many an hour we fantasize about rustic scenes of unalloyed bliss; oh! and about you! How often must she pay homage to you; must not, does so willingly, is so glad to hear about you, loves you.—

Oh, were I sitting at your feet in that dear, intimate little room, and the little dears were romping around me, and if they grew too noisy for you, I would gather them around me and quiet them with a spine-chilling fairy tale.

The sun is setting gloriously over a countryside gleaming with snow, the storm has passed, and I—have to lock myself in my cage again.—Adieu! Is Albert with you? And how—? God forgive me this question!

FEBRUARY 8

For the past week we have had the most abominable weather, and it is good for me. Because for as long as I've been here, there has not been one beautiful day in the sky that someone hasn't spoiled or ruined for me. If now it rains hard and blows and freezes and thaws—ha! I think, it can't be any worse in the house than it is outside, or vice versa, and so all is well. If the sun rises in the morning and promises a fine day, I can never resist crying out: There they have another gift from heaven that they can ruin for each other! There is nothing that they do not ruin for each other. Health, reputation, joy, recreation! And for the most part out of silliness, lack of understanding, and narrow-mindedness, and, to hear them tell it, with the best of intentions. Sometimes I feel like falling on my knees and begging them not to tear themselves to pieces in such fury.

FEBRUARY 17

I'm afraid that my ambassador and I will not be able to stand each other much longer. The man is completely intolerable. His way of working and waging business is so ridiculous that I can't help contradicting him and often doing the thing according to my lights and in my fashion, which then, of course, he cannot accept. For this reason he has recently complained about me at the Court, and the Minister has reprimanded me, gently, to be sure, but it was still a reprimand, and I was on the point of tendering my resignation when I received a private letter[†] from him, a letter to which I bowed down

† Out of respect for this excellent gentleman, this letter and another one mentioned below have been removed from this collection, because we do not feel that such an impropriety could be excused even by the warmest gratitude of the public. (Note by Goethe's "Editor.")

and whose lofty, noble, wise intelligence I worshiped. How he rebukes my excessive sensitivity, how, of course, he ascribes my high-minded ideas about efficiency, influencing others, and succeeding in business to youthful high spirits; and though he honors them and has no wish to eradicate them, he seeks only to tone them down and to guide them to where they can truly come into play, have the most powerful effect. And so I have been strengthened for the past eight days and become one with myself. Calmness of soul is a splendid thing and a joy in itself. Dear friend, if only the jewel were not every bit as fragile as it is beautiful and precious.

FEBRUARY 20

God bless you, my dear ones, and give you all the good days of which He deprives me.

I thank you, Albert, for deceiving me: I waited for news of when your wedding day would be, and I had resolved to take down Lotte's silhouette most solemnly from the wall on that day and bury it under other papers. Now you are married, and her picture is still here! Well, so it shall remain! And why not? I know I am with you both, and without injury to you, I am in Lotte's heart, indeed I hold the second place there and want to and must keep it. Oh, I would go mad if she could forget—Albert, hell lies in that thought. Albert, farewell! Farewell, angel from Heaven! Farewell, Lotte!

MARCH 15

I have been so greatly vexed that I may be driven away from here. I'm gnashing my teeth! The devil take it! It cannot be made good, and it's all your fault, you who spurred me on and drove me and tormented me to take a position that was not what I wanted. Now I've got mine! now you have yours! And so you won't say again that it's my high-minded ideas that ruin everything, here you have, my dear sir, the narrative, plain and unadorned, the way a chronicler would write it down.

Count von C. is fond of me, favors me—that is a known fact, that is something I've told you a hundred times. Yesterday I was invited to dinner at his home, the self-same day when in the evening the noble company of gentlemen and ladies, to whom I've never given a thought, meets at his house, nor did it ever occur to me that we underlings do not belong there. Very well. I eat with the Count, and after the meal we walk up and down in the great hall, I speak with him, with Colonel B., who joins us, and so the hour for the assemblage approaches. God knows that I suspect nothing. Thereupon there enters the excessively gracious Lady von S. with her husband and thoroughly hatched little goose of a daughter, with her flat chest and dainty laced bodice, and widen en passant their exaltedly noble eyes and flare their nostrils as tradition dictates, and as this class of people disgusts me to the core, I was about to take my leave, waiting only until the Count was rid of their obnoxious prattle, when my Fräulein B. arrived. As my heart always leaps up a little when I see her, I stayed put and took my stand behind her chair; it was only after a while that I realized she was speaking to me less freely than usual, with some embarrassment. I was struck by this. Is she, too, like all these people? I thought, and was stung and wanted to go, and yet I stayed because I would have been glad to forgive her and did not believe what was happening and still hoped for a kind word from her and—what have you. In the meantime the company was filling up. Baron F. in a wardrobe dating in its entirety from the coronation of Francis the First; Court Councilor R. but here, in view of his status, titled Herr von R. with his deaf wife, etc.; never forgetting the ill-dressed J., who patches the holes in his old-fashioned wardrobe with newfangled rags. They come up in twos and threes, and I speak with several persons of my acquaintance, who are all very curt. I thought—and attended only to my B. I did not register that the women at the end of the room were whispering into each other's ears, that the whispers circulated among the men, that Frau von S. was speaking with the Count (all that was told me afterward by Fräulein B.), until finally the Count came up to me and drew me into a window niche.—You are familiar, he said, with our wonderful conditions; the company is displeased, I notice, to see you here. I would not want under any circumstances—Your Excellency, I interrupted, a thousand pardons; I should have thought of it sooner, and I know you will forgive me this lapse; I meant to leave a while ago. An evil genius held me back, I added, smiling, as I bowed.—The Count squeezed my hands with an emotion that said it all. I slipped quietly away from the distinguished company, went out, got into a cabriolet, and drove to M——, there to watch the sun set from the hill and read in my Homer the splendid scene where Ulysses enjoys the hospitality of the excellent swineherd. All that was well and good.

In the evening I return for supper; there were only a few people in the taproom, playing dice on one corner of the table: they had turned the cloth back. Then the honest A. comes in, puts down his hat, and catching sight of me, walks up and says quietly, Have you had a bad time?—I? I said—The Count ordered you out of the company.—The Devil take it! I said, I was glad to get out into the fresh air—It's good, he says, that you're taking it so lightly. The only thing that annoys me is that it's already all over the place.—That's when the thing really began to get under my skin. Everyone who came to the table and looked at me made me think: He's looking at you because of that! It made my blood boil.

And today, everywhere I turn I am pitied, and I hear that those who are jealous of me are now triumphant, saying:

There you see where the arrogant end up, those who think themselves superior on account of their scrap of intellect and believe that this entitles them to rise above the conventions, and more of the same low drivel—then you feel like thrusting a knife into your heart; because you can speak of independence as much as you like, but show me the man who can bear to have scoundrels talk about him when they have an advantage over him. When their blather is harmless, oh, then it's easy to ignore them.

MARCH 16

Everything conspires against me. Today I met Fräulein B. on the avenue; I could not refrain from talking to her, and as soon as we were at some distance from the others, I revealed my pain at her recent behavior—Oh Werther, she said to me in a tender tone, how could you interpret my confusion this way, you who know my heart? How I suffered for you from the moment I came into the room! I foresaw the whole thing, a hundred times it was on the tip of my tongue to tell you. I knew that von S. and von T. and their husbands would sooner leave than remain in your company; I knew that the Count was in no position to spoil things between them—and now the commotion!—How is that, Fräulein? I said, concealing my dismay, because at that moment everything Adelin had said to me the day before was rushing through my veins like boiling water—What it has already cost me! said the sweet creature as tears came to her eyes—I could no longer control myself, I was about to throw myself at her feet.—Explain yourself! I cried.—Tears streamed down her cheeks. I was beside myself. She dried them, without attempting to conceal them.—You know my aunt, she began, she was present and saw it, oh, with what a look! Werther, I had to get through the night, and this morning I had to endure a sermon about associating with you and had to listen to her denigrate, demean you, and I could and might only half defend you.

Every word she spoke pierced my heart like a sword. She did not realize what a mercy it would have been to conceal all of it from me, and now she went on to add the gossip that would be spread and the sort of people who would now gloat. How they would be tickled and delighted at the retribution for my arrogance and my scathing opinion of others, for which they had long reproached me. To hear all that, Wilhelm, from her, in a tone of the most genuine sympathy—I was shattered and am still furious inside. I wanted someone to dare to reproach me, so that I could run him through with my rapier; the sight of blood would make me feel better. Oh, a hundred times I have seized a knife to relieve this constricted heart of mine. I have heard about a noble breed of horses which, when they are terribly overheated and agitated, instinctively bite open a vein in order to breathe freely. This is how I often feel, I'd like to open a vein that would grant me eternal freedom.

MARCH 24

I have asked the Court for my dismissal and will, I hope, receive it, and you will forgive me for not asking your permission first. I simply had to go away, and I already know everything that you would say to persuade me to stay, and so—Break it gently to my mother, I can't help myself, and she will have to accept the fact that I cannot help her either. Of course, it will pain her. To see her son's brilliant career, just at its beginning and leading to privy councilor and ambassador, come to a stop and now . . . back, little ox, into your stall! Make what you will of this and figure out the possible conditions under which I could have and should have stayed; enough, I'm leaving; and so that you may know where I'm heading, there is a Prince *** here who finds my company to his liking; he heard of my decision to resign and has asked me to accompany him to his estates and enjoy the beauties of spring there. I am to be left entirely to my own devices, he promised, and as we do understand one another up to a point, I intend to take my chances and go with him.

APRIL 19

FOR YOUR INFORMATION

Thanks for both your letters. I did not reply because I left this page blank until my departure from the Court was at hand; I was afraid that my mother might apply to the Minister and make it more difficult for me to carry out my plan. But now it is done, my release is here. I won't tell you how reluctantly my leave was granted and what the Minister wrote me—you would burst into renewed lamentations. The Crown Prince sent me twenty-five ducats as a going-away present, along with a note that has moved me to tears; and so I will not need the money from my mother for which I recently asked her.

MAY 5

I'm leaving here tomorrow, and because my birthplace is only a detour of six miles from my route, I want to see it again, want to recall the old days I happily dreamed away there. I will enter by the very gate through which my mother drove out with me when, after my father's death, she left that dear, familiar place to confine herself in her unbearable town. Adieu, Wilhelm, you will hear of my journey.

I have completed the nostalgic journey to my hometown with all the reverence of a pilgrim, and I was gripped by many unexpected emotions. I had the coach stop at the great linden tree that stands a quarter of an hour's drive from the town on the road to S——, got out, and had the coachman drive on so that I could savor every memory on foot in a wholly new way, vividly, to my heart's content. Now I found myself standing under the tree that, when I was a boy, had been the end point and the boundary of my walks. What a difference! At that time, in blissful ignorance, I longed to set out into the unknown world, where I hoped to find so much that would nourish my heart, so much pleasure to fill and gratify my striving, yearning breast. Now I have returned from the great world—oh, my friend, with how many shattered hopes, with how many ruined plans!—I saw rising before me the mountains that had been the object of my longing a thousand times over. I could sit here for hours, yearning to be on the other side, losing myself with all my heart and soul in the woods, the valleys that appeared to my eyes in so inviting a twilight; and when the hour approached that I had to return, with what reluctance I would leave that dear place!—I drew nearer to the town; I greeted all the old familiar garden houses, I heartily disliked the new ones, as I did all the other changes that had been made. I walked through the gate and found myself at once, wholly and completely. Dear friend, I do not wish to go into detail; as charming as it was for me, it would become just as tedious in the telling. I had intended to stop at the market square, right next to our old house. On the way I noticed that the schoolroom, where an honest old woman had cooped up our childhood, had been converted into a small store. I remembered the restlessness, the tears, the dullness of mind, the anxiety I had endured in that hole.—I took no step that was not remarkable. A pilgrim in the Holy Land does not encounter so many places laden with religious recollections, and his soul is hardly so full of holy emotion.—Just one example from a thousand. I walked downstream along the river toward a certain farm; that used to be one of my walks and one of the spots where we boys practiced producing the greatest number of skips as we sailed flat stones across the water. I remembered so vividly how I sometimes stood and watched the water, the wondrous intimations with which I followed it, how full of adventure I imagined the regions to which it flowed, and how quickly I reached the limits of my imagination; and yet the movement had to continue, had to go farther, always farther, until I was completely lost in contemplation of an invisible distance.— You see, my dear friend, just so limited and so happy were the splendid patriarchs! just so childlike were their feelings, their poetry! When Ulysses speaks of the immeasurable sea and the infinite earth, it is so true, human, intensely felt, confined, and mysterious. What use is it to me that now, along with every schoolboy, I can parrot that the Earth is round? Man needs only a few clods of earth to enjoy life, fewer to rest beneath it.

Now I am here, at the Prince's hunting lodge. It is easy to get along quite well with the gentleman, he is sincere and uncomplicated. He is surrounded by some peculiar people, whom I cannot understand at all. They don't seem to be rascals, and yet they do not have the look of honest men. Sometimes they seem honest to me, and yet I cannot trust them. What pains me further is that he often speaks of matters he has only heard or read about and always from the exact standpoint that some other person has presented to him.

He also values my mind and my talents more than he does

this heart of mine, which is the sole object of my pride, the only source of everything, all my strength, all my bliss, and all my wretchedness. Oh, anyone can know what I know—my heart belongs to me.

MAY 25

I had something in mind that I didn't want to tell you about until it was carried out: Now that nothing will come of it, I may as well tell you. I wanted to go off to war; my heart had been set on it for a long time. It was chiefly for this reason that I followed the Prince, who is a general in the service of ***. When we took a walk together, I disclosed my intention to him; he advised against it, and it would have had to be more of a passion than a whim of mine had I refused to listen to his reasons.

JUNE 11

Say what you want, I cannot stay here any longer. What am I supposed to do here? Time hangs heavy on my hands. The Prince treats me as well as anybody can, and yet I am not in my element. Basically we have nothing in common. He is a man of reason but of a quite ordinary sort of reason; his companionship is no more entertaining than a well-written book. I'll stay another week and then set off into the blue again. The best thing I've done here is my drawing. The Prince has a feeling for art and would have an even deeper feeling if he were not limited by that vile academicism and its conventional terminology. Sometimes I gnash my teeth when, my imagination taking fire, I lead him through nature and art, and he suddenly thinks he's done the correct thing by bumbling in with a stock technical term.

JUNE 16

Yes, truly, I am nothing more than a wanderer, a pilgrim on this earth! You, then—are you anything more?

JUNE 18

Where is it that I mean to go? Let me tell you in confidence. I must remain here for two more weeks after all, and then I've deluded myself into thinking that I want to visit the mines in ——, but really, there's nothing to that, I just want to be nearer to Lotte, that's all. And I laugh at my own heart—and do its bidding.

JULY 29

No, it is well! All is well!—I—her husband! Oh God, Who created me, if You had granted me this bliss, my whole life would be one continuous prayer. I have no wish to contend with You, and pardon me these tears, pardon me my vain desires!—She, my wife! If I had taken into my arms the dearest creature under the sun—a chill runs through my whole body, Wilhelm, when Albert grasps her around her slender waist.

And, do I dare say it? Why not, Wilhelm? She would have been happier with me than with him! Oh, he is not the man to fulfill all the desires of that heart. A certain lack of sensibility, a lack—make of it what you will; that his heart does not beat sympathetically at—Oh!—at the passage in a favorite book where my heart and Lotte's beat as one; as on a hundred other occasions when it happens that we voice our feelings about the behavior of some third person. Dear Wilhelm!—

Certainly, he loves her with all his soul, and what doesn't that sort of love deserve?

—An unbearable fellow has interrupted me. My tears have dried. I am distracted. Adieu, dear friend.

AUGUST 4

I am not the only one to whom this happens. All men are disappointed in their hopes, deceived in their expectations. I visited that good woman under the linden trees. Her oldest boy ran up to meet me, his shouts of joy brought out his mother, who looked very dejected. Her first words were: Good sir, alas, my Hans is dead!—He was the youngest boy. I was silent.— And my husband, she said, returned from Switzerland empty-handed, and if it were not for some good folk, he would have had to beg his way home, he caught a fever traveling.—There was nothing I could say, and I gave the little boy something; she asked me to accept a few apples, which I did, and I left this place of sad memories.

AUGUST 21

The ease with which we turn over a hand: that's the way I change. Sometimes a joyous glimpse of life makes an effort to flicker into existence again, alas, for only a moment!—When I lose myself in dreams, I can't resist the thought: What if Albert were to die? You would! Yes, she would—and then I pursue this fantasy until it leads me to the brink of abysses from which I recoil with a shudder.

When I walk out of the gate, along the road I took the first time to fetch Lotte for the dance, how utterly different things were! Everything, everything, has gone by! No hint of the world as it was, no pulse-beat of my earlier emotion. I feel as a ghost must feel who returns to the burned-out ruins of a castle he, as a prosperous prince, built and appointed with all the articles of splendor and, full of hope, bequeathed to his beloved son on his deathbed.

SEPTEMBER 3

Sometimes I cannot understand how someone else *can* love her, *is allowed to* love her, when I love her so exclusively, so intensely, so fully, and recognize nothing nor know nor have anything but her!

SEPTEMBER 4

Yes, it is so. As nature declines into autumn, it is becoming autumn in and around me. My leaves are turning yellow, and the leaves of the neighboring trees have already fallen. Didn't I once write you about a peasant boy, just after I came here? Now I've inquired about him again in Wahlheim; I was told that he had been driven out of his job, and no one claimed to know anything more about him. Yesterday I met him by chance on the way to another village, I spoke to him, and he told me his story, which moved me doubly and triply, as you will easily understand when I recount it to you. But what is the point, why don't I keep to myself something that frightens and sickens me? Why should I trouble you as well? Why do I always give you the opportunity to pity me and chide me? Let it be: this too might be an element of my fate!

With a quiet sadness, in which I seemed to detect some shyness, the fellow at first only answered my questions; but very soon more openly, as if he had suddenly recognized himself and me, he confessed his missteps and lamented his misfortune to me. My friend, if only I could put every one of his words before you for your judgment! He admitted, indeed, he told me, with a sort of pleasure and happiness at remembering again, that his passion for his employer had grown day by day, so that finally he did not know what he was doing, unable, as he expressed it, to know where to lay his head. He could not eat or drink or sleep, something seemed stuck in his throat, he did things he should not have done, he forgot the chores that were assigned to him, it was as if he were pursued by an evil demon until, one day, when he knew that she was in an upstairs room, he followed her, or rather, something pulled him to her. When she refused to listen to his pleas, he tried to take her by force; he did not know what had come over him, and as God was his witness, his intentions toward her had always been honorable, and there was nothing he had desired more fervently than that she should marry him and spend her life with him. After he had spoken for a while, he began to stammer, like someone who still has more to say but does not trust himself to bring it out; finally he further confessed shyly the little intimacies she had allowed him and the familiarity she had granted him. He broke off two or three times and repeated, protesting forcefully, that he was not saying this to run her down, as he expressed it, that he loved her and held her in high esteem as before, that he had never told a soul such things and that he was only telling me so as to convince me that he was not depraved or out of his mind.—And here, dear friend, I begin to strike up my old refrain, which I will sing eternally: If I could only present the man to you as he stood before me, as he continues to stand before me! If I could only tell you everything properly, so that you could feel how I sympathize, cannot help but sympathize with his fate! But it is enough, since you also know my fate, also know me, you know all too well what draws me to all unfortunates, and especially to this unfortunate man.

As I reread this page, I see that I have forgotten to tell

you the end of the story, but it can easily be supplied. She resisted him; enter her brother, who had hated the young man for a long time, who had long wished him turned out of the house, because he feared that if his sister remarried, his children would be deprived of the inheritance, which, since she is childless, gives them high hopes. The brother immediately threw the boy out of the house and raised such a hue and cry about the matter that the woman could not have taken him back even had she wanted to. Now she has taken on another hired hand, and it's said that she has quarreled with her brother about him as well; it's claimed for certain that she will marry him, but my lad is firmly determined not to live to see that.

What I am telling you is not exaggerated, in no way prettified, indeed, I may even call it weak, I have told it weakly, and coarsened it by telling it in words taken from our traditional moral vocabulary.

This love, this loyalty, this passion, then, is no poetic invention. It is alive, it exists in its purest form in that class of people that we call uncultivated, that we call crude. We cultivated people—malcultivated into nothing! Read this story with reverence, I beg you. I am calm today as I record it; you can tell from my handwriting that I do not swoop and swirl in my usual fashion. Read it, my dear friend, and as you do, think that it is also your friend's story. Yes, this is what happened to me, this is what will happen to me, and I'm not half so good, not half so determined as this poor wretch, with whom I hardly dare to compare myself.

SEPTEMBER 5

She had written a note to her husband in the country, where he is staying on account of business. It began: My best, my dearest love, come back as soon as you can, I look forward to your return with a thousand joys.—A friend who arrived brought the news that certain circumstances would prevent Albert from coming back soon. The letter was not sent, and in the evening it fell into my hands. I read it and smiled; she asked me why?—What a divine gift imagination is! I exclaimed; for a minute I could pretend that it had been written to me.—She broke off, my words seemed to displease her, and I fell silent.

SEPTEMBER 6

It cost me effort before I could bring myself to put away the plain blue dress coat in which I danced with Lotte for the first time, but lately it had become quite shabby. And I've ordered another one made just like it, with collar and lapels, and the same kind of yellow waistcoat and trousers to go with it.

It doesn't have quite the same effect, though. I don't know—I think in time I might begin to like it better.

SEPTEMBER 12

She had been away for a few days to bring Albert back. Today I walked into her room, she came to meet me, and I kissed her hand with a thousand joys.

A canary flew from the mirror onto her shoulder.—A new friend, she said, and coaxed him onto her hand, he's a present for my little ones. Isn't he a darling! Look at him! When I give him bread, he flutters his wings and pecks at the crumb so daintily. He kisses me too, watch!

As she held out her mouth to the little creature, it snuggled up so charmingly to her sweet lips, as if it could feel the bliss it was being granted.

I want him to kiss you too, she said and handed me the bird.—The little beak made the trip from her mouth to mine, and the pecking sensation was like a breath, an intimation of love's delights.

His kiss, I said, is not entirely without greediness, he is looking for food and turns away, dissatisfied by the empty caress.

He also eats out of my mouth, she said.—She offered him a few crumbs with her lips, from which the joys of innocent, sympathetic love smiled with perfect delight.

I turned my face away. She should not be doing this! should not tease my imagination with these images of heavenly innocence and bliss and wake my heart from the sleep into which the monotony of life sometimes lulls it!—And why not?—She trusts me! She knows how much I love her!

SEPTEMBER 15

It could drive you mad, Wilhelm, that there are people without any sense or feeling for the few things on earth that still matter. You know the walnut trees under which I sat with Lotte at the home of the good pastor at St. ——, the splendid walnut trees! that, God knows, always filled my soul with such great pleasure! How cozy a place they made of the parsonage, how cool! And how splendid the branches! And the memories, back to the good clergymen who planted them so many years ago. The schoolmaster often spoke one name, which he had heard from his grandfather; he was said to have been such a fine man, and his memory was always sacred to me beneath the trees. I tell you, the schoolmaster had tears in his eyes as we spoke yesterday about how they had been chopped down—chopped down! I could go into a rage, I could murder the dog who struck the first blow. I, who would mourn without end if such a pair of trees stood in my yard and one of them were to die of old age, I have to see this happen. Dear heart, there's one good thing! What is called human feeling! The whole village is muttering, and I hope the deficit in butter and eggs and other signs of trust will make the pastor's wife aware of the wound she has inflicted on her village. For *she* is the one, the wife of the new pastor (the old one died as well), a skinny, sickly creature who has every reason to take no interest in the world, since no one is interested in her. A fool, who pretends to be learned, meddles in the investigation of the canonical books, spends a great deal of time and effort on the moral-critical reformation of Christianity that is so fashionable and shrugs her shoulders at Lavater's raptures, is in severely broken health, and hence takes no joy in God's earth. Only such a creature found it possible to chop down my walnut trees. You see—I can't get over it! Imagine, the falling leaves sully her yard, leaving it musty, the trees rob her of daylight, and when the nuts are ripe, the boys throw stones at them, and that gets on her nerves, that disturbs her in her profound reflections, when she weighs Kennikot, Semler, and Michaelis against each other. As I saw how dissatisfied the village people were, especially the older ones, I asked: Why did you put up with it?—When our mayor wants something, they said, what can you do?—But one thing turned out right. The mayor and the pastor—who also wanted to profit from the vagaries of his wife, who in no way adds to his daily enjoyment—thought of sharing the profits; but then the Treasury learned of the business and demanded: Give it here! because it still has some old entitlements to the part of the parsonage where the trees had stood, and it sold them to the highest bidder. There they lie! Oh, if I were the Prince! I would have the pastor's wife, the mayor, and the Treasury—Prince!— Indeed, if I were the Prince, what would I care about the trees on my lands?

OCTOBER 10

I need only see her black eyes and I feel so well! You
see, what vexes me is that Albert does not seem as happy as
he—hoped—as I—thought I would be—if—I do not like
introducing dashes, but in this instance I cannot express
myself otherwise—and I do, I think, express myself clearly
enough.

OCTOBER 12

Ossian has driven Homer from my heart. What a world
into which this splendid poet leads me! To roam across the
heath, amid the howling of the gale that, through the steamy
mists, sweeps along the ghosts of forefathers in the twilight
of the moon. To hear, coming from the mountains, amid
the roar of the forest stream, the groans, half blown away,
of the spirits from their caverns, and the lamentations of the
maiden grieving herself to death at the four gravestones,
moss-covered and overgrown with grass, of one who is nobly
fallen, her beloved. Then, when I find him, the wandering,
gray-haired bard who seeks the footsteps of his forefathers on
the broad heath and, alas, finds their gravestones and then,
wailing, looks up at the lovely evening star, which hides itself
in the rolling sea; and a past time lives again in the hero's soul,
a time when the friendly light still illuminated the dangers
of the brave and the moonshine illuminated their garlanded
ship returning victorious; when I read the grave sorrow on his
brow and see the last abandoned splendid wraith, exhausted,
stagger to his grave, how he forever absorbs new, painfully
ardent joys in the impotent presence of the shades of his
departed loved ones and looks down at the cold earth, at the
tall, bending grasses, and cries out: The wanderer will come,

will come, he who has seen me in my beauty, and will ask:
Where is the bard, Fingal's excellent son? His footsteps pass
over my grave, and he asks in vain for me on this earth.—O
my friend! I would, like a noble bearer of arms, draw my
sword and release my prince from the convulsive torments of
a slowly dying life at one stroke and send my soul to follow the
liberated demigod.

OCTOBER 19

Alas, this void! This dreadful void that I feel in my
breast!—I often think: If you could press her to your heart
just once, just once, the entire void would be filled.

OCTOBER 26

Yes, I am growing certain, dear friend, certain and ever
more certain, that the existence of any one creature matters
little, very little. A woman friend came to see Lotte, and I
went into the next room to get a book, and I could not read,
and then I picked up a pen to write. I heard them talking
quietly; they were discussing trivial things, local news: how
this one was married, how that one was ill, very ill.—She has
a dry cough, her bones are sticking out of her face, and she
has fainting fits; I wouldn't give a nickel for her life, said the
one. A certain party is also in a very bad way, said Lotte.—
He's all bloated, the other said.—And my lively imagination
transported me to the bedside of these poor folk; I saw them,
saw with what reluctance they turned their backs on life, how
they—Wilhelm! And my good little women were speaking
about all this in the same way everybody speaks about it—that
a stranger is dying. And when I look around me, surrounded
by Lotte's clothes and Albert's papers everywhere, and see
this room and this furniture that is now so familiar to me,

even this inkwell, and I think, Look what you mean to this home! You are their be-all and end-all. Your friends venerate you! You often give them joy, and your heart feels that it could not exist without them; and yet—if you were to go now, if you were to leave this circle? Would they feel, how long would they feel, the void that your loss would gouge into their destiny? How long?—Oh, man is so transitory that even there, where he has a genuine certainty of his existence, there, where his presence makes its one truthful impression in the memory, in the soul of his dear ones, there too he must be extinguished, must vanish, and so soon!

OCTOBER 27

I could often rend my breast and bash my brains out when I realize how little we can mean to one another. Alas, the love, joy, warmth, and bliss that I fail to bring to another, he will not give me, and though my whole heart is full of bliss, I will not bring joy to the man who stands before me, cold and vacuous.

EVENING

I have so much, and my feelings for her swallow everything; I have so much, and without her everything turns to nothing for me.

OCTOBER 30

If I have not been on the point a hundred times of throwing my arms around her! Great God knows what it feels like to see so much loveliness flitting in front of you and not be allowed to reach for it; and reaching for things is surely the most natural of human instincts. Don't children reach for whatever comes their way?—And I?

God knows! So often I go to bed with the wish—indeed, sometimes with the hope—not to wake; and in the morning I open my eyes, see the sun again, and am miserable. Oh, if only I could be moody, could blame the weather, blame some third person, blame a failed undertaking, then only half of the unbearable burden of my naysaying would rest on me. Woe is me! I feel all too clearly that I alone bear all the guilt—not guilt! Enough that the source of all misery lies deep within me, as formerly the source of all bliss.—Am I not still the same man who at one time floated in a fullness of feeling, who was followed at every step by a paradise, who had a heart to embrace a whole world with love? And this heart is now dead, no ecstasies flow from it, my eyes are dry, and my senses, no longer refreshed by restorative tears, furrow my brow with anxiety. I suffer greatly, for I have lost what was once the sole joy of my life, the sacred, life-giving power with which I created worlds around me; it is gone!—When I look out my window at the distant hill as the morning sun breaks through the fog that lies upon it and illuminates the peaceful meadow, and the gentle river winds its way toward me between the leafless willows—oh! when this splendid nature stands before me as rigid as a lacquered miniature, and all the glory cannot pump one drop of happiness from my heart into my brain, and this fellow here stands before the countenance of God like a well run dry, like a broken pail. I have often thrown myself on the ground and begged God for tears, like a farmer for rain when the heavens loom iron-colored above him and the earth all around him is dying of thirst.

But, alas! I feel it, God does not send rain and sunshine to our impetuous pleading, and the days whose memory torments me, why were they so blissful? if not because I awaited His spirit with patience and received the rapture that He poured over me with my entire deeply thankful heart!

NOVEMBER 8

She has reproached me for my excesses! Oh, with such charm and kindness! My excesses: that I am sometimes seduced by a glass of wine into drinking a whole bottle.— Don't do it! she said, think of Lotte!—Think! I said, do you need to tell me that? I think!—I don't think! You are always present to my soul. Today I sat at the spot where you got out of the coach the other day.—She changed the subject to stop me from delving too deeply into my theme. My dear friend, I'm beyond the pale. She can do with me as she likes.

NOVEMBER 15

I thank you, Wilhelm, for your sincere concern, your well-meant advice, and I beg you to be calm. Let me suffer to the end; despite all my weariness of life, I still have enough strength to see it through. I respect religion, you know that. I feel that it is a staff for many an exhausted soul—refreshment for many a languishing creature. But—can it, does it have to be so for everyone? When you look at the whole wide world, you see thousands for whom it was not so, thousands for whom it will not be so, whether they have been preached to or not; does it, then, have to be so for me? Does not the Son of God himself say that those shall be with him whom the Father has given to him? Now, what if I have not been given? Now, what if the Father wants to keep me for Himself, as my heart tells me?—I beg of you, do not interpret this the wrong way, do not see something like mockery in these innocent words; it is my entire soul that I am baring to you; otherwise I would have preferred to keep my silence, just as I would be happy not to waste words on matters that everyone knows as little about as I do. What is it except man's fate to suffer his measure to the end, drain his cup to the dregs?—And if the chalice was too bitter on the human lips of the God from Heaven, why should I boast and pretend that it tastes sweet to me? And why should I be ashamed in the dreaded moment when my whole being trembles between being and not-being, when the past flashes like lightning over the gloomy abyss of the future and everything around me sinks to the bottom and the world goes to ruin with me?—Is it not the voice of the creature driven entirely into itself, insufficient, and irresistibly crashing downward, who, in the inner depths of his powers, as they struggle upward in vain, gnashes its teeth and cries: My God! my God! Why hast Thou forsaken me? And should I be ashamed of this expression, should I be afraid of a moment that did not escape him who folds up the heavens like a garment?

NOVEMBER 21

She does not see, she does not sense that she is preparing a poison that will destroy both her and me; and I, with lustful pleasure, sip from the cup she hands me, to my ruination. Of what use is the kind look that she often—often?—no, not often, but indeed sometimes, gives me, the grace with which she accepts an involuntary expression of my feelings, the compassion for my suffering that is written on her brow?

Yesterday, as I was leaving, she gave me her hand and said: Adieu, dear Werther!—Dear Werther! It was the first time that she called me Dear, and it pierced me to the quick. I've repeated it to myself a hundred times, and last night, as I was about to go to bed and was chatting with myself about all sorts of things, I suddenly said, just so: Good night, dear Werther! and then I had to laugh at myself.

NOVEMBER 22

I cannot pray: Let her be mine! and yet she often seems to me to be mine. I cannot pray: Give her to me! for she belongs to another. I go around expending my wit on my pains; were I to give myself free rein, I could produce a whole litany of antitheses.

NOVEMBER 24

She feels my suffering. Today her gaze forced its way deep into my heart. I found her alone; I did not say anything, and she looked at me. And I no longer saw in her the lovely beauty, no longer the radiance of her excellent spirit; all that had disappeared from my sight. A far more splendid look affected me, the full expression of the most intense sympathy, the sweetest compassion. Why was I not allowed to throw myself at her feet? Why was I not allowed to respond by embracing her and showering her with a thousand kisses? She sought refuge at the piano and, as she played, she softly, sweetly breathed out harmonious sounds. Never have I seen her lips so enchanting; it was as if they opened to sip the sweet tones rising from the instrument, and what reverberated was only the covert echo from her pure mouth—oh, if I could only tell you, quite plainly!—I stopped resisting, bent my head, and took an oath: Never will I dare to press a kiss onto you—lips—on which the spirits of heaven flutter. And yet—I want—ha! Do you see, it stands like a rampart before my soul—this bliss—and then: Go to your destruction to expiate this sin—sin?

NOVEMBER 26

Sometimes I tell myself: Your fate is unique; count the others fortunate—no one else has ever been so tormented.— Then I read a poet from ancient times, and it seems as if I were looking into my own heart. I have to endure so much! Oh, then, can men who lived before me have been so miserable?

NOVEMBER 30

I shall, I shall not come to my senses! Wherever I turn, I encounter an apparition that destroys my composure. Today! O destiny! O mankind!

I went down to the water at noon, I did not feel like eating. Everything was bleak, a moist, cold west wind was blowing in from the mountain, and gray rain clouds were moving into the valley. At a distance I saw a man in a shabby green coat clambering among the rocks, apparently looking for herbs. As I approached and he turned on hearing the noise I made, I saw an interesting physiognomy, whose main feature was a quiet mournfulness but which otherwise expressed nothing more than good, honest sense; his black hair was pinned into two rolls, with the rest woven into a thick braid that hung down his back. Since his clothes seemed to mark him as a member of the lower class, I felt certain that he would not be offended if I took notice of his doings, and I asked him what he was looking for.—I am looking, he replied, sighing deeply, for flowers—and I cannot find any.—It isn't the right time of year for them, I said, smiling.—There are so many flowers, he said as he walked down to join me. In my garden there are roses and two kinds of woodbine, my father gave me one of them, they grow like weeds; I've been looking for two days and can't find them. But out here there are always flowers, yellow and blue and red, and the centaury has a pretty little flower. I can't find any at all.—I detected something weird and therefore I asked in a roundabout way, Why do you want the flowers?—A strange, quivering smile twisted his face.—If you won't tell anyone, he said while pressing a finger to his lips, I promised my sweetheart a posy.—That's good of you, I said.— Oh! he said, she has a lot of other things, she's rich—And yet she'd love a posy from you, I replied.—Oh! he continued, she has jewels and a crown—What's her name?—If the States-General would only pay me, he replied, I'd be a different man! Oh yes, there was a time when I felt very happy! But now I'm done for. Now I'm—a tearful glance at the heavens expressed it all.—So you were happy? I asked.—Oh, I wish I were that way again! he said. I felt so wonderful, so joyful, as light as a fish in water!—Heinrich! called an old woman who was walking toward us, Heinrich, where are you hiding? We've been looking for you everywhere, come to dinner!—Is that your son? I asked, as I went over to her—Yes, my poor son! she replied. God has given me a heavy cross to bear.— How long has he been this way? I asked.—It's been six months now, she said, that he's been so calm. Thank God that he's only this far gone, earlier he was raving mad for a whole year, they put him in chains in the madhouse. Now he wouldn't harm a soul, except he's forever got kings and emperors on the brain. He was such a good, calm boy, he helped support me, he had such beautiful handwriting, and then all of a sudden he became broody, came down with a burning fever, went from there into raving madness, and now he's the way you see him. If I were to tell you, sir—I interrupted the flow of her words with the question, What was that time, the time when he boasts of having felt so happy, so wonderful?—The foolish boy! she exclaimed with a pitying smile, he means the time when he was out of his mind, he always boasts of it; that's the time he was in the madhouse, when he had no idea who he was.—That left me thunderstruck, I pressed a coin into her hand and hurriedly left her.

When you were happy! I exclaimed to myself, walking quickly straight toward town, when you were as happy as a fish in water!—God in Heaven! Have You so designed men's fate that they are happy only before they arrive at reason and after they lose it!—Poor wretch! and yet, how I envy your melancholy, the confusion of your senses in which you languish! You are filled with hope as you set out to pluck flowers for your queen—in winter—and mourn when you cannot find any and fail to understand why you cannot find any. And I—and I go out without hope, without purpose, and return home the way I came.—You imagine what sort of man you would be if the States-General paid you. Blessed creature! who can attribute his lack of happiness to an earthly obstacle! You do not feel! you do not feel that your misery lies in your shattered heart, in your ravaged brain, and all the kings in the world cannot help you recover. Let that man die a hopeless death who mocks the afflicted man journeying to the farthest healing spring, which will only add to his ills and render what remains of his life more painful! who looks down on the harried heart of the man who goes on a pilgrimage to the Holy Sepulcher to rid himself of the scruples of his conscience and to cast off the sufferings of his soul. Every step that cuts into the soles of his feet on the untrodden path is a drop of balm for his anguished soul, and with every day's march that he endures, his heart lies down to rest relieved of many of its afflictions.—And you dare to call that madness, you, on your soft pillows, you phrasemongers?—Madness!— Oh God! You see my tears! Must You, who created man sufficiently poor, also give him brothers who would rob him of the bit of privation, the bit of trust he has in You, in You the All-Loving One! For the trust in a healing root, in the tears of the vine—what is that except trust in You, trust that You have placed in all that surrounds us the power to heal and alleviate which we need in every hour of our life? Father! Whom I do not know! Father, Who once filled my entire soul and now has turned His countenance away from me! call me to You! be silent no longer! Your silence will not halt this thirsting soul—and could a man, a father, be angry with his son who, returning unexpectedly, throws his arms around him and cries out: I've come home, Father! Do not be angry that I have broken off my journey when it was your will that I should have endured longer. The world is the same all over, after effort and labor come recompense and joy; but what has that to do with me? I am happy only where You are, and it is in your countenance that I want to suffer and enjoy.—And you, dear Father in Heaven, would You cast him from You?

DECEMBER 1

Wilhelm! The man I wrote you about, that fortunate unfortunate, was a clerk in the office of Lotte's father, and it was a passion for her, which he nourished, concealed, revealed, and for which he was dismissed, that drove him mad. As you read these dry words, feel with what derangement of my senses I was gripped by the story, which Albert told me with just as much composure as you may be feeling as you read it now.

DECEMBER 4

I beg of you—You see, I am done for, I can bear it no longer! Today I was sitting with her—I sat, she played the piano, various tunes, and so much expression! so much!— so much!—What would you have me do?—Her little sister was dressing her doll on my knee. Tears rose to my eyes. I bent my head and caught sight of her wedding ring—my tears flowed—and all at once she began to play the old, the heavenly, the sweet melody, just all at once, and a consoling feeling ran through my soul, and a memory of all that was past, of the times when I had heard the tune, the gloomy intervals, my chagrin, my failed hopes, and then—I paced up and down the room, my heart choking from the stress.—For God's sake, I said, starting toward her with a violent outburst, for God's sake, stop! She stopped and looked fixedly at me. Werther, she said, with a smile that pierced my soul, Werther, you are very ill, all your favorites do not agree with you! Go! I beg of you, calm down.—I tore myself away from her and— God! You see my misery and You will put an end to it.

DECEMBER 6

How her image pursues me! Waking and dreaming, it fills my entire soul! Here when I close my eyes, here inside my head, where the lines of my inner vision join, I find her black eyes. Here! I cannot describe it to you. When I close my eyes, they're there; like an ocean, like an abyss, they lie before me, in me, filling the senses inside my head.

What is man, the celebrated demigod! Does he not lack strength precisely where he needs it most? And if he soars upward in joy or sinks down in sorrow, will he not be arrested in both, just there, just then, brought back to dull, cold consciousness when he was longing to lose himself in the fullness of the infinite?

The Editor to the Reader

How DEVOUTLY I wish that enough documents in his own hand concerning the last remarkable days of our friend had been left to us so as to render it unnecessary for me to interpose my narrative in the sequence of the remaining letters.

I have gone to great lengths to collect accurate reports from the lips of those in a position to be well acquainted with his history; it is a simple one, and all accounts of it are in agreement, barring a few insignificant details; it is only about the cast of mind of the persons closely involved that opinions differ and judgments diverge.

What can we do but relate conscientiously all that we were able to glean after repeated efforts, intercalating the letters the departed left behind, never neglecting the slightest slip of paper we found, especially given the difficulty of discovering the truly genuine, the authentic motives behind even a single action when it is found among persons who are not of the common stamp.

Indignation and displeasure became more and more deeply rooted in Werther's soul, growing ever more tightly entangled and gradually taking possession of his entire being. The harmony of his mind was completely devastated, an internal heat and violence, which labored to confuse all his natural powers, produced the most repellent effects and finally left him with nothing but an exhaustion from which he sought to rise with even greater anxiety than when he had struggled with all the woes of his past. The dread in his heart sapped his remaining intellectual strength, his vivacity, his wit; he became a sorry companion, always more unhappy, and always more unfair the unhappier he grew. At least Albert's friends say as much; they claim that Werther—who, so to speak, consumed his total assets every day, only to suffer want and deprivation in the evening—was not competent to judge a blameless, quiet man who had arrived at the happiness he had long yearned for or to question the manner in which he sought to preserve his happiness in the future.—Albert, they say, had not changed in so short a time; he was still the same man whom Werther had known from the beginning, whom he had so highly esteemed and respected. He loved Lotte more than anything in the world, he was proud of her and wanted to have her acknowledged by everyone as the most splendid of women. Hence, could he be blamed for also wanting to avoid every trace of suspicion at a moment when he had no desire to share his exquisite possession with anyone, even in the most innocent fashion? They admit that Albert often left his wife's room when Werther was with her, but not out of hatred or aversion for his friend, but simply because he felt that Werther was inhibited by his presence.

Lotte's father had fallen ill and was confined to his room; he sent his carriage for her, and she drove out to him. It was a fine winter's day, the first heavy snow had fallen, covering the region.

The next morning Werther followed, so that if Albert did not come for her, he might escort her home.

The clear weather did little to affect his cheerless mood, a dull weight pressed on his soul, mournful images lodged firmly in his brain, and his mind knew no other motion than to veer from one excruciating thought to the next.

As he lived with himself in perpetual strife, the condition of others appeared to him only more problematic and convoluted; he believed that he had destroyed the beautiful relationship between Albert and his wife, he reproached himself for this—and his reproaches became tempered by an element of veiled repugnance for the husband.

On his way his thoughts were occupied by this subject as

well.—Yes, yes, he said to himself, surreptitiously gnashing his teeth, here we have that intimate, friendly, tender, all-encompassing companionship, that serene, enduring faithfulness! It is satiety, and it is indifference! isn't it true that every paltry business transaction means more to him than his precious, exquisite wife? Can he appreciate his good fortune? Can he respect her as she deserves? He has her, all well and good, he has her—I know that, just as I know something else: I think that I've become accustomed to the thought, it will drive me mad, it will kill me—and has his friendship for me continued? Doesn't he already see in my affection for Lotte an interference with his rights, in my attentiveness to her a silent reproach? I know it well, I feel it, he is not glad to see me, he wants me to go away, my presence is a burden to him.

He often slackened his pace, he often stood still and seemed inclined to turn back; but each time he aimed his steps forward, and finally, with such thoughts and soliloquies, he arrived, so to speak against his will, at the hunting lodge.

He entered and asked after the old gentleman and Lotte; he found the house in considerable uproar. The oldest boy told him that there had been a calamity in Wahlheim, a peasant had been killed!—It made no real impression on him.—He entered the sitting room and found Lotte trying to dissuade the old gentleman, who in spite of his illness insisted on going to Wahlheim to investigate matters on the spot. The perpetrator was still unknown, the body had been found that morning outside the door of his house, there were suspicions: the murdered man was the servant of a widow who had previously employed another man who had left the house after a dispute.

On hearing this, Werther started up vehemently.—Can it be! he exclaimed, I have to go there, I can't wait another moment.—He hurried toward Wahlheim, every memory vivid in his mind, and he did not doubt for a moment that the young man with whom he had spoken a few times and whom he had come to like so much had committed the crime.

As he had to walk under the linden trees to get to the tavern where they had laid the body, he was appalled by the spot he had formerly cherished so deeply. That threshold, where the neighbors' children had so often played, was stained with blood. Love and loyalty, the most beautiful of human sentiments, had turned into violence and murder. The powerful trees stood without foliage and covered with hoarfrost; the beautiful hedgerows, which arched over the low wall of the churchyard, had lost their leaves, and the snow-covered headstones could be glimpsed through the gaps.

As he approached the tavern, before which the entire village was gathered, shouting suddenly broke out. A troop of armed men could be seen at a distance, and the crowd shouted that they were bringing in the murderer. Werther saw the man and was no longer in doubt. Yes, it was the young servant who had loved that widow so much and whom he had met some time ago wandering around in quiet fury and secret despair.

What have you done, you wretched man! Werther cried out as he went up to the prisoner.—The latter looked at him quietly, was silent, and finally replied quite calmly, No one will have her, she won't have anyone.—The prisoner was brought into the tavern, and Werther rushed away.

This terrible, violent upheaval threw everything in his nature into confusion. For a moment he was wrested from his sadness, his dejection, his indifferent acceptance; a resolute sympathy took possession of him, and he was seized by an inexpressible urge to save the man. He felt him to be so unlucky, found him so innocent even as a criminal, and put himself so completely in his place that he fully believed he could persuade others as well. He wished he were able to speak at once in the man's defense, the most vivid speech was already rushing to his lips; he hurried to the hunting lodge and on the way could not refrain from voicing under his breath everything he wanted to say to the District Officer.

When he came into the sitting room, he found Albert there; this spoiled his mood for a moment; but he soon took hold of himself and declared his convictions in fervent tones. The District Officer shook his head several times, and although Werther, with the greatest vivacity, passion, and truth, set forth everything a man can say in defense of another man, the District Officer, as can easily be imagined, remained unmoved. On the contrary, he did not allow our friend to finish speaking, hotly contradicted him, and rebuked him for protecting an assassin; he pointed out to him how, in this way, every law would be abrogated, the security of the state would be destroyed; he added that in such a case there was nothing he could do without taking upon himself the gravest responsibility; everything had to proceed in an orderly manner, according to the prescribed procedure.

Werther did not give up yet but asked only that the District Officer look the other way if the man should be helped to escape! This suggestion, too, was rejected. Albert, who finally joined the discussion, also took the part of the old gentleman. Werther was outvoted, and suffering furiously, he went away after the District Officer had told him several times, No, he cannot be saved!

How deeply these words must have struck him we can see from a note found among his papers, a note that had certainly been written that same day:

"You cannot be saved, you wretched man! I see all too well that we cannot be saved."

What Albert had said in the end, in the presence of the District Officer, about the prisoner's case had been extremely offensive to Werther; he thought he had detected in it a certain annoyance with him, and even if, upon further reflection, it did not escape his critical judgment that both men might be right, he nevertheless felt as if he would have to renounce his innermost being in order to admit it, to concede it.

A note referring to this matter, which perhaps expresses the entirely of his relation to Albert, is found among his papers:

"What good does it do me to tell myself, and tell myself again, that he is fine and good, it nevertheless tears my innermost entrails to pieces; I cannot be fair."

Because it was a mild evening, and the weather was beginning to tend to a thaw, Lotte walked home with Albert. On the way she looked around here and there, as if she were missing Werther's company. Albert began to speak about him, he criticized him while doing him justice. He touched on Werther's unfortunate passion and wished that it might be possible to send him away.—I wish it for our sake as well, he said, and I beg you, he continued, to make an effort to give his conduct toward you a different direction, to make his visits less frequent. People are beginning to notice, and I know that there's been talk about it here and there.—Lotte was silent, and Albert appeared to have registered her silence: at least from that time on, he no longer mentioned Werther to her, and when she mentioned him, he let the conversation drop or changed the subject.

Werther's one vain attempt to save the unfortunate man was the last flare of the flame of a light on the brink of extinction; he sank ever deeper into pain and lethargy; in particular, he was almost beside himself when he heard that he might be summoned to testify against the hired hand, who was now taking refuge in denial.

Every unpleasantness that he had ever encountered in

his active life—the vexation at the embassy, whatever else he had failed to accomplish, whatever had ever unsettled him—rose and fell in his soul. As a result, he found himself entitled to lethargy, he found himself cut off from any prospect, incapable of grasping any handle to take hold of life's ordinary affairs; and so, finally, given over entirely to his strange feelings, his way of thinking, and his endless passion, in the eternal monotony of a sad companionship with the lovely and beloved creature whose calm he disturbed, raging against his powers, exhausting them without purpose or prospect, he moved ever closer to a sorry end.

Several of the surviving letters are the strongest testimonies to his confusion and passion, his restless doing and striving, and his weariness with life; we will include them here:

DECEMBER 12

Dear Wilhelm, I am in the state that must have been experienced by those unfortunate creatures who were thought to be ridden by an evil demon. At times it takes hold of me; it is not terror, not lust—it's an unfamiliar inner frenzy that threatens to rip my breast apart, that constricts my throat! Woe! Woe! and then I roam through the frightful night scenes of this hostile season.

Last night I felt compelled to go outside. A thaw had suddenly set in; I had heard that the river had overflowed its banks, all brooks were swollen and my dear valley flooded from Wahlheim down! In the night, after eleven o'clock, I ran outside. A frightful spectacle: to see the rushing floodwaters whirling down from the rocks in the moonlight, over fields and meadows and hedgerows and all around, and up and down the wide valley a single raging lake in the howling of the wind! And then, when the moon came out again and rested over the black clouds, and down below me the floodwaters rolling and pounding in the awesome, splendid reflection: a shudder came over me and again a longing! Oh, with my arms wide open I stood facing the abyss and breathed down! down! and was lost in the bliss of hurling my torments, my suffering raging down! roaring away like the waves! Oh!— and lifting your foot from the ground and ending all your torments—that was beyond you!—My hour has not yet come, I feel it! Oh, Wilhelm! How gladly I would have given up my human existence to be with that stormy wind and tear the clouds apart and seize the floodwaters! Ha! And might that bliss not be bestowed on this imprisoned creature one day?—

And as I looked down in my melancholy at a spot where I had rested with Lotte under a willow tree after a warm walk— that too was flooded, and I could hardly discern the willow! Wilhelm! And her meadows, I thought, the grounds around her hunting lodge! our bower devastated by the smashing stream! I thought. And the sunbeam of the past peered in, like a prisoner's dream of flocks, meadows, and honorific posts! I stood there!—I do not reproach myself, for I have the courage to die.—I could have—now I sit here like an old woman who gleans her wood from fences and her bread at people's doors to ease and prolong her waning, joyless life one moment longer.

DECEMBER 14

What is this, my dear friend? I frighten myself! Isn't my love for her the most sacred, chaste, brotherly love? Has my soul ever felt a punishable desire?—I will not declare—and now, dreams! Oh, how truthfully those men felt who attributed such contradictory effects to alien powers! Last night! I tremble as I say it, I held her in my arms, pressed tightly against my breast, and covered her mouth, which whispered of her love, with never-ending kisses; my eyes swam in the intoxication of hers! God! Is it an offense for me to feel this bliss even now as I recall these fervent joys with full intensity? Lotte! Lotte!—And I am done for! My senses are confused, a week ago I lost all reasoning powers, my eyes are filled with tears. Nowhere do I feel happy, and I feel happy everywhere. I wish for nothing, ask for nothing. It would be better for me were I to go.

During this time, under such conditions, the decision to leave this world had gathered greater and greater strength in Werther's soul. Since his return to Lotte it had always been his final prospect and hope; yet he had told himself that it must not be a hurried, a rash act; he wanted to take this step with absolute conviction, with the calmest possible determination.

His doubts, his quarrel with himself are evident in an undated note that is probably the beginning of a letter to Wilhelm found among Werther's papers:

Her presence, her fate, her sympathy with mine squeeze the last tears from my scorched brain.

To lift the curtain and step behind it! That is all! And why this hesitation, this loss of heart? Because there is no knowing what lies behind it, and there is no coming back? And that it is a quality of our mind to have a foreboding of confusion and darkness wherever we have no definite knowledge.

Finally, he became ever more accustomed to and familiar with the sad thought, and his resolution grew firm and irrevocable, to which the following ambiguous letter he wrote to his friend attests:

DECEMBER 20

I have your love for me, Wilhelm, to thank for understanding my words as you did. Yes, you are right: it would be better for me if I went away. I don't really like your suggestion that I return to all of you; at least I should like to make a detour, especially since we have reason to hope for lasting frost and good roads. I am also deeply appreciative of your wanting to come for me; just wait another fortnight and expect a letter from me with more details. It is vital not to pluck anything before it's ripe. And a fortnight more or less can make a big difference. I'd like you to tell my mother that she must pray for her son and that I ask her forgiveness for all the vexation I have caused her. It was my fate to grieve those to whom I owed joy. Farewell, my dearest friend! May all the blessings of heaven be upon you! Farewell!

What transpired in Lotte's soul during this time, what her convictions were toward her husband and her unfortunate friend, we scarcely venture to put into words, though given our knowledge of her nature, we can surely form an implicit idea, and a beautiful feminine soul can think its way into hers and feel as it does.

This much is certain: she was firmly resolved to do all she could to send Werther away, and if she hesitated, it was from a sincere, friendly desire to spare him, because she knew how much it would cost him, indeed, that he would find it almost impossible. Yet, during this time she began to feel a greater urgency to make a serious effort; her husband was completely silent about the relation, just as she, too, had always remained silent about it, and she therefore felt it all the more pressing to prove to Albert through her actions that her convictions were equal to his.

On the same day—it was the Sunday before Christmas— that Werther had written his friend the letter inserted above, he visited Lotte in the evening and found her alone. She was busy arranging some toys that she had prepared as Christmas presents for her little sisters and brothers. He spoke about the pleasure the children would enjoy, and of the times when the unexpected opening of a door and the apparition of a decorated tree with wax lights, sweetmeats, and apples would produce paradisiacal rapture.—You too, said Lotte, concealing her embarrassment behind a charming smile, you too shall have a present if you're on your best behavior—a wax candle and something else.—And what do you mean, if you're on your best behavior? he exclaimed; how shall I be? How can I be? dearest Lotte!—Thursday evening, she said, is Christmas Eve, the children will come, my father as well, everyone will get a present, you'll come too—but not before.—Werther was taken aback.—I beg you, she continued, that is the way it must be, I beg you for the sake of my peace, it cannot, it cannot go on this way.—He turned his eyes away from her and walked up and down the room, muttering her phrase between his teeth: It cannot go on this way! Lotte, who felt the frightful state into which these words had thrown him, tried to turn his thoughts in another direction with all sorts of questions, but in vain.— No, Lotte, he exclaimed, I shall not see you again!—Why say that? she replied. Werther, you can, you must see us again, but in moderation. Oh, why did you have to be born with this vehemence, this untamed, unyielding passion for everything you touch! I beg you, she continued, taking his hand, Learn moderation! Your mind, your knowledge of so many things, your talents: what a variety of pleasures they offer you! Be a man! Find another direction for this sad devotion to a person who can only pity you.—He ground his teeth and looked at her morosely.—She held his hand: Be calm and sensible for just one moment, Werther! she said. Can't you tell that you are deluding yourself, that you are willfully destroying yourself! But why me, Werther? Me in particular, someone who belongs to another man? That in particular? I'm afraid, I'm afraid it's only the impossibility of possessing me that makes you want me so much.—He pulled his hand from hers while staring at her with a rigid, angry look.—Clever! he cried, very clever! Did that remark perhaps come from Albert? Astute! Very astute!—It can come from anyone, she replied, and in the whole world is there no girl who can fulfill the desires of your heart? Make up your mind, go look for her, and I swear to you you'll find her; for a long time now I've been worried for your sake and ours about the constraints into which you've condemned yourself lately. Make up your mind, a journey will, must distract you! Look for, find a worthy object of your love, and return and let us enjoy together the bliss of a true friendship.

—You could put that into print, he said with a cold laugh, and recommend it to every tutor. Dear Lotte! Just give me a little peace, all will be well!—Just this, Werther: You're not to come any time before Christmas Eve!—He was about to reply when Albert came into the room. The two men wished each other good evening in chilly tones, and in their embarrassment they walked alongside each other up and down the room. Werther began a trivial conversation, which soon died out; Albert did the same, then asked his wife about certain household tasks, and when he heard that they had not yet been done, spoke a few words to her that struck Werther as cold, indeed harsh. He would have liked to leave but could not and delayed until eight o'clock, his dejection and displeasure steadily increasing until the table was set and he took up his hat and walking stick. Albert invited him to stay, but he, who believed he had heard only an empty gesture, thanked him coldly and left.

He returned home, took the candle from the hand of the boy who wanted to light the way for him, and went into his room alone, wept aloud, talked excitedly to himself, walked anxiously up and down the room, and finally, still in his clothes, threw himself on the bed. There he was found by his servant, who ventured to come in about eleven o'clock to ask whether he should take off his master's boots. This Werther permitted and forbade the servant to come into the room the following morning before he was called.

Early on Monday morning, the twenty-first of December, he wrote Lotte the following letter, which after his death was found sealed on his desk and was delivered to her. I will insert it in fragments, which is how he wrote it, as the circumstances make clear.

It is settled, Lotte, I want to die, and I tell you this without romantic excesses, with composure, on the morning of the day when I will see you for the last time. When you read this, my dearest, the cold grave will be covering the rigid remains of the restless man, the unfortunate man who, in the last few moments of his life, knows no greater sweetness than to converse with you. I have spent a terrible night and, oh, a beneficent night. It is this that has made my decision firm, definite: I want to die! When I tore myself away from you last night, in the dreadful revolt of all my senses, when all of it oppressed my heart and when my hopeless, joyless existence beside you seized me with gruesome coldness—I could barely reach my room, and beside myself, I threw myself to my knees and, oh God! You granted me the final consolation of the bitterest tears! A thousand plans, a thousand prospects raged through my soul, and in the end it stood there, definite, intact, the final and only thought: I want to die!—I lay down, and in the morning, in the serenity of waking, it still stands there, definite, intact, and strong in my heart: I want to die!—It is not despair, it is the certainty that I have borne my suffering to the end and am sacrificing myself for you. Yes, Lotte! Why should I keep silent? One of the three of us must go, and I want to be the one! Oh my dearest! In this torn heart the ferocious thought has prowled, often—of murdering your husband!—you!—me!—So be it!—When you climb the mountain on a lovely summer evening, remember me, how I so often came up from the valley, and then look out toward the graveyard to my grave, where the wind sways the high grass this way and that in the glow of the setting sun.—I was calm when I began; now, now I am sobbing like a child, as all of it becomes so vivid to me.—

Shortly before ten o'clock Werther called his servant and, as he dressed, explained that he would be going on a trip in a few days and that therefore he should brush his clothes and get everything ready to be packed; he also ordered the boy to ask for all his bills, collect some books he had lent out, and as there were some poor people to whom he was accustomed to give something each week, to pay out their allotment two months in advance.

He had his breakfast brought to his room, and after the meal he rode out to the District Officer, whom he did not find at home. He walked up and down the garden in deep thought, seemingly wanting, at the end, to heap upon himself the full melancholy of memory.

The children did not leave him in peace for long; they ran after him, jumped on him, told him that, after tomorrow, and one more tomorrow, and one more day, they would get Christmas presents at Lotte's house, and they told him of the wonders that their childish imaginations anticipated.— Tomorrow! he exclaimed, and another tomorrow! and one more day!—and gave them all affectionate kisses and was about to leave when the smallest boy wanted to whisper in Werther's ear. He confided that his big brothers had written beautiful New Year's greetings, this big! And one for Papa, one for Albert and Lotte, and also one for Herr Werther; these they were going to hand out early on New Year's Day. At that, Werther felt overwhelmed, he gave something to each child, got on his horse, sent his respects to the old man, and rode away, his eyes filling with tears.

Shortly before five o'clock he arrived home and ordered the maid to look to the fire and keep it burning into the night. He asked the young servant to pack his books and linens into the bottom of his trunk and to bundle up his clothes. Then he seems to have written the following paragraph of his last letter to Lotte:

You are not expecting me! You think I am going to obey and not see you again before Christmas Eve. Oh Lotte! today or never again. On Christmas Eve you will hold this letter in your hand, tremble, and moisten it with your adorable tears. I will, I have to! How happy I feel to have come to my decision.

In the meantime Lotte had fallen into a peculiar state of mind. After her last conversation with Werther she had come to understand how difficult it would be for her to part from him and how much he would suffer if he were forced to leave her.

It had been mentioned in Albert's presence, as if in passing, that Werther would not come again before Christmas Eve, and Albert had gone off to an official in the neighborhood with whom he had business to conduct and where he would have to spend the night.

Now Lotte was sitting by herself; none of her sisters and brothers were with her. She abandoned herself to her thoughts, which silently ranged over her situation. She now saw herself bound forever to the man whose love and fidelity she knew and for whom she felt a deep affection, whose calm and reliability seemed truly heaven-sent as a foundation on which a good woman might build her life's happiness; she knew what he would always be for her and her children. On the other hand, Werther had grown so dear to her; from the very first moment of their acquaintance the harmony of their hearts and minds had been so beautifully evident; her long and unbroken companionship with him, the many situations they had experienced together, all had left a lasting impression on her heart. She had become used to sharing with him all those feelings and thoughts that were of any interest, and his departure threatened to tear open a void in her whole existence that could never be filled. Oh, if in that moment she could have turned him into a brother, how happy she would have been!—If she had been allowed to marry him off to one of her friends, if she could have hoped to reestablish his unbroken relationship with Albert.

In her mind she perused the list of her friends and found something to criticize in each one, found none whom she would have wished on him. Over and above all these considerations, for the first time she felt deeply, yet without making it clear to herself, that the secret longing of her heart was to keep him for herself; and at the same time she told herself that she could not, might not keep him; her pure, beautiful spirit, usually so light and able so easily to manage difficulties, felt the pressure of a melancholy to which the prospect of happiness is barred. Her heart was squeezed tight, and a dark cloud hung over her eyes.

And so it was half past six when she heard Werther coming up the stairs and soon recognized his step and his voice asking for her. How her heart began to beat, and for the first time, we may almost say, at his approach. She would have preferred to have him told she was not at home, and when he entered the room, she cried out to him in a sort of impassioned confusion: You did not keep your word.—I promised nothing, was his answer.—Then you should at least have granted me my wish, she replied; I asked you for the sake of your peace of mind and my own.

She did not rightly know what she was saying, any more than what she was doing when she sent for a few of her friends so she would not be left alone with Werther. He put down some books that he had brought, asked about other things, and at one moment she wished that her friends would come and at the next that they might stay away. The maid returned, bringing the message that both had sent their regrets.

She wanted to have the maid settle in the next room and do her work there; then she thought differently again. Werther walked up and down the room, she went to the piano and struck up a minuet, but the tune would not flow. She pulled herself together and sat down calmly next to Werther, who had taken his accustomed place on the settee.

Do you have nothing to read? she said.—He had nothing.—There in my drawer, she began, is your translation of some of the songs of Ossian. I have not yet read them, I had always hoped to hear them from you; but since then the occasion has never presented itself, nor could I arrange it.—He smiled, he fetched the songs, a tremor went through him as his hands held them, and his eyes filled with tears as he glanced at the pages. He sat back down and read:

"Star of descending night! fair is thy light in the west! thou liftest thy unshorn head from thy cloud; thy steps are stately on thy hill. What dost thou behold in the plain? The stormy winds are laid. The murmur of the torrent comes from afar. Roaring waves climb the distant rock. The flies of evening are on their feeble wings; the hum of their course is on the field. What dost thou behold, fair light? But thou dost smile and depart. The waves come with joy around thee; they bathe thy lovely hair. Farewell, thou silent beam! Let the light of Ossian's soul arise!

And it does arise in its strength! I behold my departed friends. Their gathering is on Lora, as in the days of other years. Fingal comes like a watery column of mist; his heroes are around. And see the bards of song, grey-haired

Ullin! stately Ryno! Alpin, with the tuneful voice! the soft complaint of Minona! How are ye changed, my friends, since the days of Selma's feast? when we contended, like gales of spring, as they fly along the hill, and bend by turns the feebly whistling grass.

Minona came forth in her beauty; with downcast look and tearful eye. Her hair flew slowly on the blast that rushed unfrequent from the hill. The souls of the heroes were sad when she raised the tuneful voice. Often had they seen the grave of Salgar, the dark dwelling of white-bosomed Colma. Colma left alone on the hill, with all her voice of song! Salgar promised to come; but the night descended around. Hear the voice of Colma, when she sat alone on the hill!

COLMA

It is night; I am alone, forlorn on the hill of storms. The wind is heard in the mountain. The torrent pours down the rock. No hut receives me from the rain; forlorn on the hill of winds!

Rise, moon! from behind thy clouds. Stars of the night, arise! Lead me, some light, to the place where my love rests from the chase alone! his bow near him, unstrung; his dogs panting around him. But here I must sit alone, by the rock of the mossy stream. The stream and the wind roar aloud. I hear not the voice of my love! Why delays my Salgar; why the chief of the hill, his promise? Here is the rock, and here the tree! here is the roaring stream! Thou didst promise with night to be here. Ah! whither is my Salgar gone? With thee I would fly from my father; with thee, from my brother of pride. Our race have long been foes, we are not foes, O Salgar!

Cease a little while, O wind! stream, be thou silent awhile! let my voice be heard around! Let my wanderer hear me! Salgar! it is Colma who calls. Here is the tree and the rock.

Salgar, my love, I am here! Why delayest thou thy coming? Lo! the calm moon comes forth. The flood is bright in the vale. The rocks are gray on the steep. I see him not on the brow. His dogs come not before him, with tidings of his near approach. Here I must sit alone!

Who lie on the heath beside me? Are they my love and my brother? Speak to me, O my friends! To Colma they give no reply. Speak to me; I am alone! My soul is tormented with fears! Ah, they are dead! Their swords are red from the fight. O my brother! my brother! why hast thou slain my Salgar? why, O Salgar! hast thou slain my brother? Dear were ye both to me! what shall I say in your praise? Thou wert fair on the hill among thousands! he was terrible in fight. Speak to me; hear my voice; hear me, sons of my love! They are silent; silent for ever! Cold, cold, are their breasts of clay! Oh! from the rock on the hill, from the top of the windy steep, speak, ye ghosts of the dead! Speak, I will not be afraid! Whither are ye gone to rest? In what cave of the hill shall I find the departed? No feeble voice is on the gale; no answer half-drowned in the storm!

I sit in my grief! I wait for morning in my tears! Rear the tomb, ye friends of the dead. Close it not till Colma come. My life flies away like a dream! why should I stay behind? Here shall I rest with my friends, by the stream of the sounding rock. When night comes on the hill; when the loud winds arise; my ghost shall stand in the blast, and mourn the death of my friends. The hunter shall hear from his booth. He shall fear, but love my voice! For sweet shall my voice be for my friends; pleasant were her friends to Colma!

Such was thy song, Minona, softly blushing daughter of Torman. Our tears descended from Colma, and our souls were sad! Ullin came with his harp; he gave the song of Alpin. The voice of Alpin was pleasant; the soul of Ryno was a beam of fire! But they had rested in the narrow house;

their voice had ceased in Selma. Ullin had returned, one day, from the chase, before the heroes fell. He heard their strife on the hill; their song was soft, but sad! They mourned the fall of Morar, first of mortal men! His soul was like the soul of Fingal; his sword like the sword of Oscar. But he fell, and his father mourned; his sister's eyes were full of tears. Minona's eyes were full of tears, the sister of car-borne Morar. She retired from the song of Ullin, like the moon in the west, when she foresees the shower, and hides her fair head in a cloud. I touched the harp, with Ullin; the song of morning rose!

RYNO

The wind and the rain are past; calm is the noon of day. The clouds are divided in heaven. Over the green hills flies the inconstant sun. Red through the stony vale comes down the stream of the hill. Sweet are thy murmurs, O stream! but more sweet is the voice I hear. It is the voice of Alpin, the son of song, mourning for the dead! Bent is his head of age; red his tearful eye. Alpin, thou son of song, why alone on the silent hill? why complainest thou, as a blast in the wood; as a wave on the lonely shore?

ALPIN

My tears, O Ryno! are for the dead; my voice for those that have passed away. Tall thou art on the hill; fair among the sons of the vale. But thou shalt fall like Morar; the mourner shall sit on thy tomb. The hills shall know thee no more; thy bow shall lie in thy hall unstrung!

Thou wert swift, O Morar! as a roe on the desert; terrible as a meteor of fire. Thy wrath was as the storm. Thy sword in battle, as lightning in the field. Thy voice was as a stream after rain; like thunder on distant hills. Many fell by thy arm; they were consumed in the flames of thy wrath. But when thou didst return from war, how peaceful was thy brow! Thy face was like the sun after rain; like the moon in the silence of night; calm as the breast of the lake when the loud wind is laid.

Narrow is thy dwelling now! dark the place of thine abode! With three steps I compass thy grave, O thou who wast so great before! Four stones, with their heads of moss, are the only memorial of thee. A tree with scarce a leaf, long grass which whistles in the wind, mark to the hunter's eye the grave of the mighty Morar. Morar! thou art low indeed. Thou hast no mother to mourn thee; no maid with her tears of love. Dead is she that brought thee forth. Fallen is the daughter of Morglan.

Who on his staff is this? who is this, whose head is white with age; whose eyes are red with tears? who quakes at every step? It is thy father, O Morar! the father of no son but thee. He heard of thy fame in war; he heard of foes dispersed. He heard of Morar's renown; why did he not hear of his wound? Weep, thou father of Morar! weep; but thy son heareth thee not. Deep is the sleep of the dead; low their pillow of dust. No more shall he hear thy voice; no more awake at thy call. When shall it be morn in the grave, to bid the slumberer awake? Farewell, thou bravest of men! thou conqueror in the field! but the field shall see thee no more; nor the dark wood be lightened with the splendor of thy steel. Thou has left no son. The song shall preserve thy name. Future times shall hear of thee; they shall hear of the fallen Morar!

The grief of all arose, but most the bursting sigh of Armin. He remembers the death of his son, who fell in the days of his youth. Carmor was near the hero, the chief of the echoing Galmal. Why bursts the sigh of Armin? he said. Is there a cause to mourn? The song comes with its music, to melt and please the soul. It is like soft mist, that, rising from a lake, pours on the silent vale; the green flowers are filled with dew, but the sun returns in his strength, and the mist is gone. Why art thou sad, O Armin, chief of sea-surrounded Gorma?

Sad I am! nor small is my cause of woe! Carmor, thou hast lost no son; thou hast lost no daughter of beauty. Colgar the valiant lives, and Annira, fairest maid. The boughs of thy house ascend, O Carmor! But Armin is the last of his race. Dark is thy bed, O Daura! deep thy sleep in the tomb! When shalt thou awake with thy songs? with all thy voice of music?

Arise, winds of autumn, arise; blow along the heath! streams of the mountains, roar! roar, tempests, in the groves of my oaks! Walk through broken clouds, O moon! show thy pale face, at intervals! bring to my mind the night when all my children fell; when Arindal the mighty fell; when Daura the lovely failed! Daura, my daughter! thou wert fair; fair as the moon on Fura; white as the driven snow; sweet as the breathing gale. Arindal, thy bow was strong. Thy spear was swift on the field, thy look was like mist on the wave; thy shield, a red cloud in a storm! Armar, renowned in war, came, and sought Daura's love. He was not long refused; fair was the hope of their friends.

Erath, son of Odgal, repined; his brother had been slain by Armar. He came disguised like a son of the sea; fair was his cliff on the wave, white his locks of age; calm his serious brow. Fairest of women, he said, lovely daughter of Armin! a rock not distant in the sea bears a tree on its side; red shines the fruit afar. There Armar waits for Daura. I come to carry his love! She went; she called on Armar. Nought answered, but the son of the rock. Armar, my love! my love! why tormentest thou me with fear? Hear, son of Arnart, hear! it is Daura who calleth thee. Erath the traitor fled laughing to the land. She lifted up her voice; she called for her brother and her father. Arindal! Armin! none to relieve you, Daura.

Her voice came over the sea. Arindal, my son, descended from the hill, rough in the spoils of the chase. His arrows rattled by his side; his bow was in his hand; five dark-gray dogs attended his steps. He saw fierce Erath on the shore; he seized and bound him to an oak. Thick wind the thongs of the hide around his limbs; he loads the winds with his groans. Arindal ascends the deep in his boat, to bring Daura to land. Armar came in his wrath, and let fly the gray-feathered shaft. It sung, it sunk in thy heart, O Arindal, my son! for Erath the traitor thou diest. The oar is stopped at once; he panted on the rock and expired. What is thy grief, O Daura, when round thy feet is poured thy brother's blood! The boat is broken in twain. Armar plunges into the sea, to rescue his Daura, or die. Sudden a blast from a hill came over the waves; he sank, and he rose no more.

Alone, on the sea-beat rock, my daughter was heard to complain; frequent and loud were her cries. What could her father do? All night I stood on the shore. I saw her by the faint beam of the moon. All night I heard her cries. Loud was the wind; the rain beat hard on the hill. Before morning appeared her voice was weak; it died away like the evening breeze among the grass of the rocks. Spent with grief she expired; and left thee, Armin, alone. Gone is my strength in war! fallen my pride among women! when the storms aloft arise; when the north lifts the wave on high; I sit by the sounding shore, and look on the fatal rock. Often by the setting moon, I see the ghosts of my children. Half viewless, they walk in mournful conference together."

A flood of tears pouring from Lotte's eyes and freeing her anguished heart checked Werther's song. He threw the pages down, grasped her hand, and wept the bitterest tears. Lotte rested her head on her other hand and hid her eyes in a handkerchief. The emotions of both were agonizing. They felt their own misery in the fate of those noble figures, felt it together, and their tears united them. Werther's lips and eyes burned on Lotte's arm; a shudder overcame her; she wanted to distance herself, and pain and commiseration numbed her like lead. She breathed deeply to recover herself and begged him, sobbing, to continue, begged with the full voice of heaven! Werther was trembling, his heart was about to burst, he raised the page and read in a breaking voice:

"Why dost thou awake me, O gale? It seems to say: I am covered with the drops of heaven. The time of my fading is near, the blast that shall scatter my leaves. Tomorrow shall the traveler come; he that saw me in my beauty shall come. His eyes will search the field, but they will not find me."

The full force of these words fell upon the unhappy man. He threw himself down before Lotte in complete despair, grasped her hands, pressed them to his eyes, to his brow, and a foreboding of his terrible resolve appeared to fly through her soul. Her senses became confused, she squeezed his hands, pressed them against her breast, bent over him with a plaintive gesture, and their glowing cheeks touched. The world faded from them. He flung his arms around her, pressed her to his breast, and covered her trembling, stammering lips with furious kisses.—Werther! she cried in a choked voice, turning away, Werther!—and with a weak hand pushed his breast away from hers;—Werther! she cried in the collected tone of the loftiest feeling.—He did not resist, released her from his arms, and, insensate, threw himself down before her.—She tore herself upward, and in anxious confusion, trembling between love and fury, she said—This is the last time! Werther! You will never see me again.—And with the fullest look of love at the wretched man, she hurried into the next room and locked the door behind her. Werther stretched out his arms to her, did not dare to restrain her. He lay on the floor, his head on the settee, and remained in this position for more than half an hour, until a noise restored him to himself. It was the maid wanting to set the table. He walked up and down the room, and when he found himself alone again, he went to the door of the little room and called in a low voice—Lotte! Lotte! only one word more! A farewell!—She was silent. He waited and pleaded and waited; then he tore himself away, crying: Farewell, Lotte! Farewell forever!

He came to the city gate. The watchmen, who knew him, let him go out without a word. A mix of rain and snow was whirling, and it was nearly eleven o'clock when he knocked at the gate again. His servant noticed, on Werther's return home, that his master's hat was missing. He did not venture to comment, helped him off with his clothes, which were soaked through. Only much later was the hat found on a crag that overlooks the valley from the slope of the hill, and it is beyond understanding how he could have climbed it on a wet and gloomy night without plunging down.

He went to bed and slept for a long time. His servant found him writing when, the following morning, on responding to his call, he brought him coffee. Werther added the following to his letter to Lotte:

For the last time, then, for the last time I open these eyes. They shall not, alas, see the sun again, a dismal, foggy day keeps it overcast. Then mourn, Nature! your son, your friend, your beloved approaches his end. Lotte, it is a feeling without compare, and yet it is most like a dozing dream to say to yourself: This is the final morning. Final! Lotte, I have no understanding of this word—final! Do I not stand here in all my vigor, and tomorrow I will lie sprawled out and limp on the ground. To die! what does that mean? See, we are dreaming when we speak of death. I have seen more than one person die; but mankind is so limited that it cannot conceive of the beginning and end of its existence. Now still mine, yours! yours, oh beloved! And one instant—parted, separated— perhaps forever?—No, Lotte, no—How can I pass away? How can you pass away? We are, yes!—pass away!—what does that mean? That is merely another phrase! an empty noise, which my heart cannot feel. Dead, Lotte! buried in haste in the cold ground, so narrow! so gloomy!—I had a friend, a woman, who was everything to me in my vulnerable youth; she died, and I walked behind her dead body and stood at her grave as they lowered her coffin and yanked away the creaking ropes from underneath and drew them up again; then the first shovel- ful of clods rolled down, and the dreaded box gave back a dull thud, and duller and duller, and finally it was covered!— I threw myself down beside the grave—my innermost being stirred, appalled, terrified, torn, but I did not know what was happening to me—what will happen to me—To die! Grave! I do not understand these words!

Oh, forgive me! forgive me! Yesterday! It should have been the last instant of my life. Oh you angel! For the first time, for the first time without any doubts, a blissful feeling glowed in the innermost depths of my being: She loves me! she loves me! my lips still burn with the sacred fire that streamed from yours; a new, warm rapture is in my heart. Forgive me! forgive me!

Oh, I knew that you loved me, knew from the first soulful glances, from the first touch of your hand on mine, and yet, when I left you, when I saw Albert beside you, I lost heart again in feverish doubts.

Do you recall the flowers you sent me, when, at that dreadful party, you could not say a word to me or give me your hand? Oh, I spent half the night kneeling before those flowers, and they sealed your love for me. But alas! These impressions were transitory, just as the feeling of God's grace gradually wanes from the soul of the believer—a feeling once granted with the fullness of heaven by sacred, visible signs.

All that is fleeting, but no eternity shall snuff out the glowing life that I savored yesterday on your lips, that I feel in me! She loves me! This arm embraced her, these lips trembled on her lips, this mouth stammered on hers. She is mine! You are mine! Yes, Lotte, for all eternity.

And what can it mean that Albert is your husband? Husband! That would be true for this world—and for this world, a sin that I love you and would tear you from his arms and into mine? Sin? Very well, and I am punishing myself for it; I have tasted it in all its heavenly rapture, this sin, have sucked life's elixir and strength into my heart. From this moment on you are mine! mine, oh Lotte! I will lead the way! going to my Father, to your Father. To Him I will lament, and He will comfort me until you come and I fly to meet you and hold you and stay with you in never-ending embraces before the countenance of the Infinite Being. I am not dreaming, I am not delirious! Close to the grave, I see more clearly. We shall be! We shall see one another again! See your mother! I shall see her, find her, ah, and pour out my whole heart to her! Your mother, your likeness.

Just before eleven o'clock Werther asked his servant whether Albert had come back. Yes, said the servant: he had seen his horse being led along. Thereupon his master gave him an open note with the message:

"Would you lend me your pistols for a trip I plan to take? Farewell! All the best!"

The dear woman had slept little the previous night; what she had been afraid of had been settled, settled in a manner that she could neither guess at nor dread. Her blood, which normally flowed so purely and lightly, was in a feverish tumult, a thousand feelings splintered her fair heart. Was it the blaze of Werther's embraces she felt in her breast? Was it displeasure at his temerity? Was it a morose comparison of her present state with former times of wholly free and easy innocence and unclouded self-confidence? How should she confront her husband, how confess to him an occurrence that would be so easy to confess and yet one she did not dare to confess? They had kept a silence between them for so long, and should she be the first to break that silence and, precisely at an inappropriate moment, make such an untoward disclosure to her husband? She was already afraid that the mere news of Werther's visit would strike him unpleasantly, and now, in addition, this unexpected catastrophe! Could she truly hope that her husband would see all of it in the proper light, absorb all of it entirely without prejudice? and could she want him to read what was in her soul? And yet again, could she dissemble in the face of a man with whom she had always been as open and transparent as a crystal goblet and from whom she had never concealed any of her feelings nor could she ever do so? Both considerations worried her and left her at a loss; and always her thoughts returned to Werther, who was lost to her, whom she could not let go, whom she, sadly! had to leave to his own devices and who, if he were to lose her, had nothing left.

How she felt the heavy weight—although it was something she could not fully realize at that instant—of the deadlock that had come about between her and Albert. Such reasonable, such good people began to keep silent in one another's company because of certain secret differences; each brooded on his own right and on the other's wrong; and circumstances grew so entangled and exasperating that it became impossible at the crucial moment to loosen the knot that could make all the difference. Had a happy intimacy brought them closer sooner, had mutual love and forbearance quickened and opened their hearts, perhaps our friend might have been saved.

Another peculiar circumstance came into play. As we know from Werther's letters, he had never made any secret of his longing to leave this world. Albert had often disputed with him on this point, and at times it had also become a subject of conversation between Lotte and her husband. The latter, who felt a decided aversion for the deed, had often made it clear, with a sort of irritability that was otherwise foreign to his nature, that he had reason to very much doubt the seriousness of any such intention, he had even allowed himself a few jokes about it and communicated his skepticism to Lotte. On the one hand, this did calm her when her thoughts displayed the sad image to her; on the other hand, it prevented her from sharing with her husband the anxieties that troubled her at that moment.

Albert came home, and Lotte went to meet him with awkward haste; he was himself in a bad mood, his business had not been brought to a conclusion, the neighboring District Officer had turned out to be rigid and narrow-minded. The vile roads had also made him peevish.

He asked whether there was anything new, and she answered too quickly: Werther had come by last night. Albert asked if there was any mail and was told that a letter and several packets had been placed in his study. He went to that room, and Lotte remained alone. The presence of the man whom she loved and honored had made a renewed impression on her heart. The recollection of his generosity of spirit, his love and kindness, had helped to calm her, she felt a secret urge to follow him, she took her needlework and went to his room, as she often tended to do. She found him occupied with opening and reading the packets. Several seemed to contain less than pleasant news. She asked him a few questions, to which he gave curt answers, and he stood at his desk to write.

They had spent an hour together like this, and Lotte's soul grew ever darker. She sensed how difficult it was going to be for her to explain to her husband, even if he were in the best of moods, what weighed on her heart. She fell into a melancholy that inspired all the more anguish in her the more she tried to hide it and swallow her tears.

The appearance of Werther's servant threw her into the greatest embarrassment; he handed the note to Albert, who turned to his wife and merely said, Give him the pistols.—I wish him a good journey, he said to the young servant.—These words left her thunderstruck, she staggered to her feet, barely conscious of what she was doing. Slowly she went to the wall; trembling, she took down the pistols, wiped the dust from them and hesitated, and would have delayed even longer if Albert had not urged her on with a searching look. Unable to utter a word, she gave the fatal instruments to the boy, and when he had left, she gathered up her work and went to her own room in a state of the most unutterable uncertainty. Her heart foretold all manner of horrors. At one moment she was about to throw herself at her husband's feet, reveal everything to him, the events of the previous evening, her guilt, and her forebodings. The next, she could not foresee a good result from such an undertaking, the last thing she could expect was to persuade her husband to go to visit Werther. The table was set, and one of her close friends, who had come by only to ask a question, intending to leave promptly—and stayed—made the table talk bearable; they forced themselves to speak; they told stories, they put everything else out of their minds.

The boy brought the pistols to Werther, who took them from him in raptures when he heard that Lotte had given

145

them to him. He had bread and wine brought to him, sent the boy off to his dinner, and sat down to write:

They have passed through your hands, you have wiped the dust from them, I kiss them a thousand times, you have touched them: And you, celestial spirit, you favor my decision, and you, Lotte, are handing me the implement, you from whose hands I wished to receive my death, and ah! receive it now. Oh, I posed question after question to my boy. You trembled as you handed them to him, you bade no farewell.—Woe! Woe! no farewell!—Can you have closed off your heart to me because of the moment that bound me to you forever? Lotte, a millennium cannot extinguish this impression! And I feel it, feel that you cannot hate him who burns for you so fiercely.

After dinner he asked the boy to finish packing, tore up a great many papers, went out, and settled a few small debts. He came back home, once again went out by way of the gate despite the rain and into the Count's garden, roamed farther into the countryside, and as night fell, returned and wrote:

Wilhelm, for the last time I have seen field and forest and sky. Farewell to you too! Mother, dear, forgive me! Console her, Wilhelm! God bless you both! My affairs are all in order. Farewell! We will meet again, more joyously.

I have repaid you badly, Albert, and you will forgive me. I have disturbed the peace of your home, I sowed distrust between you. Farewell! I want to put an end to it. Oh, if only my death could make you happy! Albert! Albert! Make this angel happy! And may God's blessing dwell upon you!

In the evening he went on rummaging through his papers, tore up many of them, and threw them into the stove, sealed a few packets addressed to Wilhelm. They contained little essays, fragmentary thoughts, several of which I have seen; and at ten, after he had more wood laid on the fire and a bottle of wine brought to him, he told his servant to go to bed; his room, like the bedrooms of the other servants, was far out at the back. The boy lay down fully clothed so as to be on hand early in the morning; for his master had told him that the post-horses would be at the house before six o'clock.

AFTER ELEVEN O'CLOCK

Everything is so quiet around me, and my soul so calm. Thank you, God, for giving my last moments this warmth, this strength.

I go to the window, dearest! and see, and still see, a few stars of the eternal heavens through the storm clouds rushing past! No, you will not fall! the Eternal One carries you in his heart and me. I see the handle of the Big Dipper, the loveliest of all the constellations. When I used to leave your house in the evening and went out by the gate, it stood up there, facing me. With what ecstasy did I gaze at it so often! so often, with my hands raised, made it into a sign, the sacred landmark of my bliss at that moment! and even now—O Lotte, what is there that does not remind me of you! do you not surround me! and haven't I, like a child, forever unsatisfied, grabbed at all sorts of trinkets that you, my saint, had touched!

Beloved silhouette! I bequeath it back to you, Lotte, and implore you to honor it. I have kissed it passionately thousands and thousands of times, greeted it with a wave of my hand a thousand times whenever I went out or came home.

I have written a note to your father asking him to take care of my body. Two linden trees stand in the churchyard, in the rear corner near the field; that is where I want to rest. He can, he will do this for a friend. Prevail upon him, Lotte. I do not expect devout Christians to lay their bodies next to that of a poor wretch. Oh, I wish you would bury me by the wayside, or in a lonely valley, so the priest and the Levite might pass by the stone marker and make the sign of the cross, and the Samaritan shed a tear.

Here, Lotte! I do not shudder to take the cold, terrible chalice from which I shall drink the ecstasy of death! You handed it to me, and I do not waver. All! All! Thus all the wishes and hopes of my life are fulfilled! To knock so coldly, so rigidly, on death's iron gate.

That I might have had the happiness of dying for you! Lotte, of sacrificing myself for you! I would die courageously, I would die joyously if I could restore to you the calm, the bliss of your life. But alas! it has been given to only a few noble souls to spill their blood for their loved ones and by their death to kindle a new hundredfold life for their friends.

These are the clothes I want to be buried in, Lotte, you have touched them, sanctified them; I have asked this of your father as well. My soul hovers over the casket. No one is to go through my pockets. This pink bow, which you wore on your bosom the first time I saw you among your children—oh, kiss them a thousand times and tell them about the fate of their unhappy friend. The dear children! They are clustering around me. Oh, how I attached myself to you! from the first instant could not leave you!—This bow is to be buried with me. It was my birthday when you gave it to me! How I gorged myself on all of it!—Oh, I never thought that my road was meant to lead me to this place!—Be still! I beg of you, be still!—

They are loaded—the clock strikes twelve! Let it be!—Lotte! Lotte, farewell! farewell!

A neighbor saw the flash of gunpowder and heard the noise of a shot; but since there was no further sound, he paid no more attention.

At six in the morning the servant comes in with a light. He finds his master on the ground, the pistol and blood. He cries out, he touches him; no response except a death rattle. He runs for the doctors, for Albert. Lotte hears the bell, all her limbs begin to tremble. She wakes her husband, they get up; wailing and stammering the servant brings the news, Lotte falls unconscious at Albert's feet.

When the physician came to the wretched man, he found him on the ground, beyond saving, there was a beating pulse, all his limbs were paralyzed. He had shot himself in the forehead above his right eye, his brain was extruded. A vein in his arm had been opened unnecessarily, the blood ran, his breath was still coming in gasps. From the blood on the back of the armchair it could be inferred that he had accomplished the deed while sitting at the desk, had then slumped over and thrown himself convulsively around the chair. He lay feebly on his back, against the window, he was fully dressed, his boots on and wearing a blue dress coat with a yellow waistcoat.

The house, the neighborhood, the town were thrown into an uproar. Albert arrived. They had laid Werther on the bed and bandaged his forehead; his face already a dead man's, he did not move a muscle. His lungs still rattled frightfully, now with a weaker, now with a stronger sound; his end was expected at any moment. He had drunk no more than one glass of the wine. Lessing's *Emilia Galotti,* its pages opened, lay on the desk.

Let me keep silent about Albert's consternation, Lotte's grief.

The old District Officer came rushing in on hearing the news, with the hottest tears he kissed the dying man. His older sons, coming on foot, arrived soon after, they fell to the floor by the side of the bed with expressions of the most unrestrained grief, kissed his hands and his mouth, and the eldest, whom Werther had always loved best, clung to his lips until Werther had passed away and the lad was torn from him by force. Werther died at noon. The presence of the District Officer and his measures averted a riot. That night, just before eleven, he had him buried at the spot Werther had chosen. The old man walked behind the body, as did his sons; Albert was unable to. They feared for Lotte's life. Workmen carried him. No clergyman attended.

TRANSLATOR'S ACKNOWLEDGMENT

If this translation has succeeded at all, a very great debt is owed to Ruth Hein, a master stylist, who assisted me every step—better, every line—of the way with her tact and precision. We have discussed each sentence of this work: the outcome is the result of our conversation. This translation is dedicated to Ruth Hein. And as no such work is possible without real-world support, I would like to thank particularly Gary Smith and the staff of the American Academy in Berlin for their perfect generosity.